All Rights Reserved

RUSTY

Emmy Ellis

Chapter One

The man—Anna couldn't bring herself to say his name—registered that she'd spotted him through the window of Under the Dryer, the salon she managed, his aging face a picture of shock. Had he only intended to make sure it was her and hadn't expected her to clock him? How long had he been watching her? The whole time she'd been cutting hair today? Had he followed

1

her, like he had before in Manchester? Or had this been a chance encounter, him surprised he'd stumbled on her while he was out and about?

No, she didn't believe in coincidences. He must have realised she'd left Manchester and somehow found out where she'd gone. Came here. His shock was because she'd caught him staring.

She thought back to when she'd lived in her bedsit not far from here, how she'd imagined someone had watched her from outside. That strange feeling you got and couldn't explain, the hairs going up on the back of your neck. She'd put it down to her being silly because he'd popped up in her life again before she'd escaped to the East End, but now…

She blinked to check if she was seeing things — fuck, he was still there, a statue of weird stillness, as if he couldn't get his feet to move. He'd come to see her in her dreams since the last time she'd spoken to him, his pleading voice grating on her nerves. He wanted a place back in her life, his dream-self said. He wanted to make amends for what he'd done.

No one could make amends for that type of behaviour.

His cheeks flushed, and he blinked. They had a creepy stare-off session, Anna compelled to meet his gaze, like he had some kind of hold on her. Her cheeks grew hot, and she reminded herself she didn't have to put up with this. George was only a few steps away, either in the office or the staffroom. One word from her, and he'd deck this bastard,

But he hurried away, head bent. He'd put on weight since last time, didn't look so haggard, and his clothes fitted better. Had he wangled himself a job despite his criminal record? With high enough wages that he could afford London prices? The self-assured air of his younger years was gone, replaced by the kick in the teeth life had given him. Good.

She laid a hand on her chest, her heart thudding, the sound of her pulse drowning out the noises of the salon: the hum of a hairdryer, the chatter, the laughter, their lives going on as usual when hers had ground to a complete, nerve-racking halt. Why did he have to come today of all days? It was the first time she'd opened, it was meant to be a fresh start, a proper new beginning, and he'd ruined it.

She'd found her feet—or George had found them for her—and her life was at last resembling something she could be proud of instead of the shameful mess it used to be. She'd even got out of the crusty bedsit, the one with mould the landlord hadn't given a shit about. She lived in the flat upstairs now, rent-free, on hand for when The Brothers or their men came to collect the guns and whatever else they'd stored in the secret wall in the office out the back.

She was involved in something illegal by working for the twins, and she'd promised she wouldn't do that, she wouldn't be like *him*, breaking the law. But George offering her such a good deal, a big wage packet and new digs, had swayed her. When he'd laid his cards on the table in the Noodle and Tiger, she'd looked at Harper, her baby son, and knew if she didn't take this chance, she'd forever be skint and struggling. She'd made the decision to do what was best for her child.

The irony of that wasn't lost on her.

Don't draw parallels.

She craned her neck and stared through the window. The man—in her head she called him Bastard—had disappeared down the street, but he might return, try to speak to her when all the customers had left. She couldn't cope with this on her own, she refused to, not after what she'd been through as a child, so she only had one option. To go and see George, who currently babysat Harper.

She came out from behind the reception desk and smiled. Put on her professional face. Said to the other stylists she managed, "I've just got to speak to George for a bit. Can you share my remaining clients between you?"

Three women still stood outside—the shop was packed, nowhere for them to sit while they waited, although you'd think they'd want to come in where there was air-con. She thought of her little notebook, where she'd written all of her dreams for this place, extra seating in the form of a sofa high on her list. It could go down the long wall beside the reception desk. George had agreed to all of it, so it was a case of waiting for the furniture to arrive.

She walked towards the door that led to the office, pushed it open, and smiled again, despite the shock she'd just had. George had fallen asleep in an armchair with Harper on his chest. At six months old, her son loved to snuggle, but who would have thought that big bear of a man liked it, too?

Thoughts of Bastard invaded her mind and wiped her smile away. Soured her fleeting moment of pretending nothing bad had happened. She approached George, conscious he'd been looking after Harper for hours. He'd even fed him, the small Tupperware pot of food she'd blended now empty, a plastic spoon inside it on the desk, along with a fromage frais carton. Why hadn't he come and got her earlier? She could have popped Harper in the playpen. The salon had a filter system that sucked up all the hairspray and dye fumes, so he'd have been okay.

Maybe George had wanted some quiet time, a place to hide out where no one knew where he was.

She sighed, hating having to wake him, especially as he'd been so down lately, on his own rather than Greg being with him. She hadn't asked why George appeared so lost, hadn't dared. He wasn't the type to have people nosing into his business. She was curious, but it was a curiosity for another day, maybe never, as she had her own business to spill.

She shook his shoulder, hoping he didn't jolt and wake Harper. What she had to say was better done without her son crying, babbling, or needing her attention.

George opened his eyes and eased himself up. "He's only just dropped off. You said he was due a nap ages ago, but the little sod wanted to play."

"And you let him."

George flushed. "Yeah, well, he made me laugh, took my mind off things. Do you want to take him?"

She glanced at the playpen. George had already removed the toys and put a blanket in there, so she lifted Harper carefully and popped him inside. The door to the staffroom on the right stood open, so she checked the back door was locked and jerked her head in that direction.

"Want a coffee? I've…I've got to tell you something." God, it was going to be awful, saying it out loud.

He frowned and clenched his fists. "Do I need to be worried?"

"No, but I do."

"Seems like there's a problem."

"You don't know the half of it."

They went into the staffroom, George sitting at the table so he could keep an eye on Harper through the doorway. She sorted coffee pods in the Tassimo he'd insisted on providing—"I don't want any of that instant shit when I'm here!"— her nerves rioting. She'd never told a stranger about her life before. Well, not since she'd been little and had to tell the police what had gone on. She'd come back to London at the beginning of her pregnancy to put some ghosts to bed and escape Bastard, and having to explain why she was here would prove hard going. Still, if she wanted help, she'd have to bring the whole lot up—as much as she knew anyway—no matter how difficult it would be.

Coffee made, she took the cups to the table and sat kitty-corner to George.

He eyed her, head cocked, as if he could read her mind. "You've been through some shit. I can see it in your face. Saw it when we had a chat down the market and in the Noodle, too. Is it Harper's dad? You said you don't know who he is, but if you do and he needs sorting…"

"No." She held up a hand. "I wasn't lying, I *don't* know who he is. He could be one of many." She winced, revolted with herself. She'd been such a slag. "That sounds bad, but once you hear my story, you'll probably understand why I went off the rails, sleeping and drinking my way through life. Are you ready? It isn't pretty."

"Go on."

She started from her earliest memory, not surprised she painted an idyllic life at first, because to her, that's what it had been. Okay, she hadn't had friends and rarely saw anyone outside of her family, but she'd had everything she'd needed and had been privileged, the house big and full of expensive things. She'd been sheltered and overprotected, though. Then the cracks had appeared, and she watched George's face as she related them. His expressions went from horror to disgust to pity and everything in between.

"Fuck me, that was *you*?" He scrubbed a hand over his chin, the stubble rasping on his palm. "I mean…what the actual eff?"

She squirmed under his intense gaze. "So you've heard about it before?"

"Um, yeah. I'll be honest, we had you screened after I offered you the job. This shit came up, but never in a million years did I think this was you. There are a fair few Anna Barkers around, so I assumed you were one of the others."

Did she mind them screening her? Not when they ran an estate and had to cover their backs, but to know they'd discovered her previous life, and now George knew it was *her*…that was embarrassing, a legacy no one should have to carry around with them. But it wasn't her fault, she'd been innocent in it all, and she'd tried to make it right back then. She shouldn't be so hard on herself. She'd been a *kid*, for fuck's sake. Still, kid or not, guilt didn't care about that.

She sighed. "I don't know everything. You probably know more than me. I've avoided finding out the nastier details."

"I can see why. What you don't know can't hurt you."

"Hmm, so they say. I often think about who I'd have been if it wasn't for…you know, all *that*. If no one had found out what was going on. Would I still be sheltered, not allowed to leave the house? Would I have become an architect like I wanted, only I'd have done my uni course online and worked from home? I wasn't meant to be a hairdresser. That job was the last one on my list. I was destined for big things, but it didn't turn out that way."

"It turned out the way it was supposed to. If it hadn't, you wouldn't have had that little boy in there." He stared through at the playpen, sipping his coffee thoughtfully. "Listen to me. I'm going to tell you something now, and I don't want it going any further. Me and my brother, we had a shocking childhood, too. I won't go into details, but we went off the rails an' all. By the time we were fifteen, we were running round the estate like monsters, so I get why you did what you did. Anyway, skip back a few years, to our mum, what she went through. If she hadn't, we wouldn't be here today. If life hadn't gone exactly as it had, then we wouldn't have taken over the estate, my brother wouldn't have been shot, and I wouldn't have had a short, sharp kick up the backside about how precious life is—and believe me, I needed it."

She gaped at him. "What? Greg was *shot*?"

He waved away her shock. "I'm not trying to make this about me, I'm just saying that things happen for a reason, and if Greg being shot made me take a step back and assess my life, if you hadn't had Harper and assessed yours… D'you see? We're better people for it, even though what went before was fucking hard—is still fucking hard."

"I get what you're saying, but it doesn't make the past any easier to handle."

"No. There are regrets."

"Is Greg…is he okay?"

"I don't want to talk about it. Too sodding painful. Just keep it to yourself. If people know I'm running the estate on my own, they might take it upon themselves to give me some grief, know what I mean?"

She nodded.

He let out a gust of air, his cheeks inflating. "So, now I know your past, what do you need help with?"

"He's here."

"What, that bloke from Manchester you said about?"

"Yes. I've not long seen him outside, staring through the window."

George went to get up.

"He's gone," she said. "I made sure before I came to see you. But I'm scared. What does he *want*? I owe him nothing, I hate him, so what does he expect from me?"

George sat. "Maybe because he's got no one else he wants to bond with you, but he can fuck right off. If he comes back, you let me know straight away. In the meantime, tell me his real name so I can get our copper on it. I can't ask her to run a search on 'Bastard', can I."

She swallowed. "I don't even want to say it."

"How can I help if you won't tell me? Write it down or something, Jesus. Or do I need to look up the case online and find it myself?"

She went into the office and scribbled it on a piece of notepad paper, taking it back to George. "What if he's using a different name?"

"Doesn't matter. We've got a PI, Mason, he can do some digging an' all. My concern is that Bastard will come and give you hassle. What do you want me to do when I find him?"

She bit her lip. "I can't say that out loud either, although I've thought about it plenty of times."

"Kill him? That isn't a problem. He deserves that after what he's done. What a fucking wanker."

She pulled at her earlobe. "Shit, why do I feel bad about wanting him dead? I'm just as bad as *them* for thinking things like that."

"Don't even go there. Taking his life will be my pleasure. I've got some nifty medieval tools I haven't used in a while and a couple of new ones. Torture devices. I'll shove one of them right up his jacksie and twist."

The visual had her going queasy. "I…I want to be there. Is that allowed?"

"Can you handle it?"

Could she? *God knows*. "I have to know he's gone. I thought he was gone before, but he came back. I have to see it to believe it."

"Don't blame you. I felt the same about the bloke who shot Greg. I went back into that fridge and checked that every single bloke had snuffed it."

"*Fridge?*"

"Long story." He ran his hands down his face. "One you don't need to know about. You've got enough shit in your head as it is without adding that to it. Have you ever thought about finding that woman you mentioned? Rusty?"

"Yes, but I don't want to go barging into her life if it'll open old wounds. She could be struggling to forget it all as much as I am."

"True. I'll hold off looking into her, although if I remember rightly, the women involved were called Victims A, B, and C, so Mason would come to a dead end on that." He pinched the bridge of his nose. "I wish you'd told me about this sooner."

"It's not something I tend to tell people, and I didn't think I needed to say. I had no idea he'd follow me."

He finished his coffee. "What about your other family? Are they still knocking about?"

"Last time I checked, yes."

"They need stringing up."

She shrugged, staring at the drink she hadn't touched. "I'd rather just forget my time with them. I ring every so often but won't go back to Manchester. I haven't even told them I had Harper."

"Probably best. They don't sound the type you want around a baby." He stood. "Right. I'll send Will round to sit out the front in the car, and someone else will take shifts with him so you're always watched, even overnight. Make sure you set the alarm as soon as the staff have gone, all right? And if you want to go out, Will can take you. Give me your phone and I'll put his number in it. He can be your personal chauffeur."

She fetched it from her handbag, unlocked it, and handed it over. "Thank you. For doing this."

He thumbed the screen. "It'll give me something to do to keep me occupied. I'm like a spare part without Greg and— Anyway, enough of that." He placed her phone on the table. "I'll go and stand out the front, message Will. I won't leave until he's here and you've been introduced."

He walked out, shoulders straight, chest puffed up, as if helping her out *was* just what he needed. Had Greg died? Had it been kept hush-hush, a funeral held on the quiet? Anna hadn't seen him for two weeks so…

Christ, poor George.

Chapter Two

After introductions had been made between Will and Anna, George got in the BMW and automatically glanced to the passenger seat to natter to his brother about what had gone on. The sharp sting of loneliness fizzled through him, and he blinked away the prickle of tears. Going around on estate business was shit without Greg, but he had no choice.

He kept having flashbacks about that fridge in the abattoir, how his twin had been gunned down. How *stupid* they'd been for not putting bulletproof vests on—something George would wear all the time now. It was uncomfortable beneath his white shirt, and something he'd never wanted to put on before, thinking it made him look weak, but that had been a pathetic ego thing, something he wouldn't indulge in again. From now on, he'd be more careful. He'd lost his devil-may-care attitude, where he thought they were invincible and nothing could ever happen to them. Cocky, that's what he'd been, Greg the one offering words of caution. Words George usually ignored. The worst had happened, and those seconds when he'd stared at Moon dragging Greg to safety would stay with him forever. In his dreams—or were they nightmares?—George relived seeing Lincoln pumping on Greg's chest to revive him. The scream George had directed at the ceiling, one that had ripped at his throat, always played as the soundtrack, over and over.

"Fuck this."

He dashed at his eyes. Crying wouldn't change things. Doing what Greg wanted would. Running the estate, avoiding answering anyone who asked where he was. Bunch of nosy bastards. He'd make sure things ran smoothly. Keep his mind busy. If he didn't have work, he'd go fucking mental, tormenting himself with what-ifs.

He messaged their copper, Janine, asking if she had time to meet him in person—or more like ordering her to find the time. Even she didn't know what had happened to Greg, barely anyone did, not even Mum's best friend. George had been putting it off, letting them know. Telling people meant opening himself up to vulnerability when he wasn't ready, allowing them to see his soft side, even softer than the one he wanted people to see. The side where he broke down and sobbed because what had happened was so unfair and he felt guilty about it.

It should have been me.

His phone bleeped.

JANINE: YOU'VE CAUGHT ME LEAVING WORK. SLOW DAY. SEEMS NO ONE WANTED TO KILL ANYBODY TODAY. MEET AT THE NOODLE?

GG: IT'D BE BETTER TO GO INTO THE REAR CAR PARK AND TALK IN ONE OF OUR CARS SO WE'RE NOT OVERHEARD.

She'd have Cameron with her, the bodyguard they'd assigned to her, and he let her know he'd get the chef to do takeaway food so they could eat while chatting. He needed a Pot Noodle to comfort him anyway.

Been eating a lot of those lately.

Greg was the chef in their house, and George missed his concoctions.

Janine and Cameron wanted curry, so he drove to the pub and parked, going inside to place the order. Nessa Feathers, the forty-something manager they'd employed, revealed her tombstone teeth to him as he marched up to the bar, her blonde hair tucked into a messy bun. She'd done well with this place, he couldn't fault her. She'd been a tough-as-nails barmaid all her working life, so her father suggesting her as a manager had been a good idea.

"All right, George?" She peered over his shoulder pointedly. "No Greg again?"

"Nope."

She stared, waiting for more.

He didn't give it.

She flashed her mammoth teeth again. "Okay, what can I get you?"

"Takeaway Pot Noodle and tiger bread, plus two of those chicken curries, both with naan bread and onion bhajis."

She prodded the till to set up the order. He frowned.

"Having company for dinner?" she asked.

He didn't like her being such a nosy tart. Anger surged. She ought to think on if she thought she could get too familiar. She was an employee, not a fucking listening ear, someone he wanted to natter to. "What's it got to do with you?"

She shrugged, unperturbed by his scowl, her smile returning. Or was she hiding the fact the tone of his question had upset her?

"Just making conversation," she said. "Isn't that what you asked me to do when I took the job? Be friendly, get people coming back?"

"Yeah, well, you sound like you're fishing for info. Change your approach."

"Had a bad day?"

He glared. "How about you don't be overly friendly to me for the time being because I'm not in the mood. We'll get along better that way."

Although aware he was being a dick, he wasn't about to back down. She'd set him off on the defensive by mentioning no Greg, and it had

21

wound him up. She wasn't to know that was a sore subject, but still, fucking hell… He thought of her father, Dickie, formerly known as the Beast during Ron Cardigan's reign, how, if Nessa told him George had just snapped at her, he'd go off on one. George had no fucks to give on that score. He didn't like Dickie, never had, and when he and Greg had taken over Cardigan, he'd been one of the first people they'd sent off to retirement. He looked forward to Dickie trying to have a pop at a future date; it'd give him an excuse to let his fists fly and teach the old man that Ron's type of gangster was out of date. Stale.

He paid her, since she'd run the order through the till instead of doing a freebie like usual, and filed that mistake away for mentioning later. He wandered over to a couple of men in suits, just finishing their dinner.

"How was the grub?" he asked.

One of them looked up at him and paled. "Lovely. Brilliant. Really nice."

"I didn't ask because I wanted you to lick my arse by praising the food even if it *isn't* nice, I genuinely want to know in case I want to try it." He eyed the sauce around the bowls. "What was it, the new carbonara?"

"Yes."

"Cheers for the feedback." He returned to the bar. "Order me a couple of those carbonara efforts an' all, please, and three bottles of Coke. *Don't* put it through the till this time. And give those two fannies over there a free pint each. Blue ties, black suits."

Nessa raised her chin, not giving him her usual smile, then got on with her job. A smidgen of guilt swam through him. Dickie was always nasty to her, and George had just done the same. He ought to apologise, do the right thing.

"I didn't mean to bark," he said. "I've had a tough couple of weeks."

"It doesn't matter."

"It does. I shouldn't have treated you like shit. You're a good woman."

She blushed. "Blimey, first time for everything, I suppose."

"What do you mean?"

"A bloke saying sorry to me."

"Is your old man still at it? Bullying you?"

She shrugged. "He'll never stop."

"If you need me on that front, give me a bell."

She nodded and walked off to pour the pints.

He leaned on the bar and swept his gaze over the customers. The place was packed, full of people enjoying themselves after work. It was getting a bit of a name for itself, and a lot of that was down to Nessa.

She took the pints over to the men who held the glasses aloft at George, appearing chuffed they were apparently 'in' with a Brother. George smiled, nodded as if they were best mates now, then turned his back on them. One of the bar staff came from out the back and glanced up and down. Spotting him, she carried a brown paper bag containing the takeaway, and he took it, thanking her.

"See you when I see you, Nessa," he called and fucked off out.

Round the back, he checked all the cars. Janine's and Cameron's sat side by side next to the BMW. He strolled over there and slid into the back seat of Janine's. Cameron sat in the passenger side, his cheeks pink.

George stared at them. "Have you two been having a cheeky snog or summat?"

Janine cleared her throat. "Of course not. Bloody hell!"

"Hmm." George fished in the bag and handed them their polystyrene trays, their meal names written on the top. He passed over plastic spoons and forks plus the small bags containing their naans and bhajis.

"Cheers," Cameron said. "I'm bloody starving."

George, impressed the chef had put a proper rubber lid on his noodle pot to save it spilling, made a mental note to pat him on the back. He took his bread and a carbonara package out and placed them on the seat beside him.

"Fuck me, you're hungry," Janine said over her shoulder.

"Been busy. Looking after a baby is hard work."

"A baby?" She choked on a piece of naan. "You?"

"What's wrong with that?"

"Nothing…"

They ate in silence for a while.

"So what's the problem?" Janine twisted so she could see him.

"I'd like to give you the abridged version, but you need to hear it all." He dished out the bottles of Coke. Noodles and bread gone, he tucked in to his carbonara. "They were right. Lovely, brilliant, really nice."

"What the fuck are you on about?" Janine asked.

"Doesn't matter." In between eating, he told her Anna's story.

"I know that case," Janine said.

"Yeah, well, some bloke's come back to upset her." He gave her the name. "I want you to poke into him, see if you can find out where he's spent any money in London so we can work out where he's staying or living."

"Right. And what excuse will I give when it comes up on the system? Oh, don't worry about answering. I forgot, that's my problem to sort out."

"Come on, Janine, don't be a cow about it. She's nervous as hell."

"I can see why. That case was…brutal."

"Yeah, Mason said something similar when we asked him to look into Anna. I didn't think *she'd* be the girl, though."

"So she's back in London, you said. Running your salon."

"Yeah."

"How is she?"

"What, apart from crapping her knickers? Fine. Getting her life back together. She's got Harper to think about now."

"Her baby?"

"Yeah."

"Okay, I'll go back to the station after this, make out I forgot to finish off some paperwork."

"Good. I need that fucker in the warehouse."

"Oh, you're going *that* far?"

"Of course I fucking am! Refresh yourself on the details while you're at it, then you'll understand why he needs to be sorted."

"I don't need to." She opened her Coke and sipped.

George packed his empty tray and pot away, swiping breadcrumbs off the seat. "I'll be off then. You two can get back to your kissing."

"We *weren't*," Janine said, teeth gritted.

"Bollocks."

George laughed and got out, taking the takeaway bag with him. He drove home, smiling to himself. Janine fancied Cameron, it was obvious. He'd never known her have a bloke, she'd said they were too much hassle and she wasn't interested. But things changed, and he reckoned she deserved a bit of happiness.

Don't we all.

Chapter Three

*O*n Friday evening, the July sun still roasting, Rusty walked up the balmy street, anxious to get to the house on time. She needed this job, the money would pay for her university clothes come September, not to mention all the pens and textbooks on the list. All she needed was three hundred—she was good at rooting out bargains from charity shops. They struggled—Dad leaving them years ago had seen to *that, plus Mum's nasty habit—and life at home was full of robbing Peter to pay Paul. Oh, and empty tummies every so often if Mum spent all her benefits on booze. And her moods, cold one minute, overly warm the next, and every other emotion in between.*

Rusty was tired of it. The constant living on a knife edge, wondering what Mum would get up to next. What she'd say, do. Whether someone would come knocking on the door to have it out with her, Rusty having to calm irate people down. She shouldn't have to live like this, worn out and wishing she'd been born to different parents.

She sighed. She could see why Dad had left and wished he'd taken her with him. She wouldn't have missed her mother much, nor their smelly, messy house. But he had a new family and didn't want to see her, which had got her thinking he didn't love her enough to bring her into his new life, that he'd tarred her with the same brush as Mum—a pain in the arse and someone to be discarded.

She could admit their family of three hadn't exactly been the best, nans and grandads, aunts and uncles giving them a wide berth because Mum liked the drink a bit too much, but it had been all Rusty had back then, the only thing that had given her stability, regardless of the chaos, the rows, the bickering. Since it had been splintered apart, all she had was Mum to cling to, and as the years had rolled by, it had become clear that she had to grow up fast in order to look after herself. Mum wasn't usually in any fit state to do it, more focused on her next drink than whether her daughter had everything she needed.

Rusty switched her mind off the past and plonked herself back into the present, the heat hot on the back of her neck. The Cline housing estate stood out from the others around here—no mattresses in front gardens, no cars at the kerbs with wheels missing, and definitely no women gossiping on doorsteps. She imagined the kids, noticeably absent, probably taking the NO BALL GAMES signs seriously, weren't the type to dick about outside, causing a nuisance, not like the ones on her estate. Decent vehicles sat on driveways, the lawns nice and short, flowers bobbing in their beds from the slight breeze. A welcome breeze. It had been bloody hot this summer, the sun wreaking havoc with Rusty's fair skin. That's what came of being a redhead, so Mum had said, freckles multiplying if Rusty stayed outside for too long.

"You've got that ginger bastard of a father to thank for that."

Rusty planned to dye her hair once she got to uni.

She hadn't told Mum about the job. She'd ask for the money and spend it on drink as soon as it had been earned. Rusty wanted the buying of clothes to be a surprise. She'd show Mum what she'd bought, proud of herself for helping, and Mum wouldn't have to worry about that particular issue anymore—one of many she didn't have the energy for, nor the inclination to get involved in. It seemed as soon as Dad had walked out, the woman had given up on her parental duties.

Rusty wished she'd stopped growing years ago so she didn't need new clothes and shoes, but it seemed she stood in over-fertile soil, her legs going on for miles. Colt's legs, Mum called them, belonging to an eighteen-year-old who wasn't like any other. Rusty didn't go in for all that makeup and boys lark, she preferred to study or read.

A bookworm, another one of Mum's names for her.

"You should get yourself a fella so you're not stuck in this dump for the rest of your life," Mum had slurred then swigged from a vodka bottle.

"I don't want a fella."

"They're the only thing that will get you anywhere, my girl."

"No, my education will."

And what Mum had said was bollocks anyway. Dad had buggered off pretty sharpish once he'd found another bird stupid enough to have him, so he hadn't exactly got Mum anywhere, had he, except up the duff and on the bottle so she could blot out the life he'd handed to her.

Rusty should feel sorry for her really. Mum had been brought up to rely on a man and hadn't got the gist that in today's world, you had to take care of yourself. Mum still slept with blokes like they were going out of fashion, thinking that out of the many frogs she kissed, one of them had to be a prince. Every time, they proved they were only after her for paid sex, and for days she'd wander around, disillusioned, vodka in one hand, a fag in the other.

She'll die from too much booze one of these days.

Was Rusty cruel to hope that happened? She'd gone past caring whether she was. There was only so much a kid was expected to take. She was a woman now, eager to cast off her life and begin a new one.

She approached number seventeen, sunlight glinting off the shiny windows, the rooms beyond hidden by closed Venetian blinds. The house, a Victorian, had three floors, maybe four, going by the tops of windows poking up from the grass. A cellar, wine likely filling it—that was how posh this street was—the panes blanked out with white paint, or maybe it was that stuff Mrs Deacon down the road used when she decorated, so no one could see what she was doing inside. She liked to hold "reveal" coffee mornings when it was done, inviting everyone in to admire the paintwork and wallpaper.

Rusty never wanted to turn into someone like that, but if she stuck around, she would.

Mr and Mrs Flemington—that's what the man had said they were called when Rusty had phoned about this job—owned a Porsche, the low-slung kind, metallic-grey, its tyres recently changed if she was any judge. Barely any grit filled the treads, the rubber pure black at the edges. She took a deep breath and walked up the drive, skirting the car so her bag didn't scrape against it. She couldn't be doing with damaging it and getting into trouble.

A golden dragon's head had been mounted on the red front door, a bell push on the jamb to the right. She rapped the knocker and held her breath. Her nerves spiked, and she had the absurd need to run and not come back. Mum also sarcastically called her Daisy Detective because Rusty's intuition was spot-on when it came to pointing out her mother was off her tits on booze—she didn't need to be a detective to know that, the slurred words and bloodshot eyes told the story all by themselves. Should she listen to it now? Run and not stop until she got home?

The door swung open, and an elegant blonde woman smiled at her, hair swept back in what Rusty guessed was a French pleat, her bright-red lips full on the bottom and thinner on top. Her fitted scarlet dress shimmered with sequins and showed off her hourglass figure, her matching high heels giving her a few inches of extra height. Rusty gawped in awe, then experienced a familiar emotion—that she didn't fit in here, the same as at school and college. Her soul somewhat diminished by this lady, she felt scabby and what Mrs Flemington would most likely call scum. A rough child. One of the unwashed.

The need to run grew stronger.

"Ah, the babysitter?" Mrs Flemington smiled, her teeth perfect and white. She glanced across the street then up and down it. Seemingly satisfied about whatever she was checking for, she put her attention back on Rusty and tilted her head. "Won't you come in?"

"Um, err..." Rusty stepped from foot to foot, her anxiety rising. Was it just that this was her first job as a babysitter and that Mrs Flemington was so beautiful making her feel this way? Or was it something more?

The woman smiled again. "Oh, I'm so sorry. Have I got you mixed up with someone else?"

"No, I'm the babysitter. I spoke to your husband on the phone."

"Rusty, isn't it? I do like a nickname."

Rusty only answered to her real name at college, she'd be the same when she went to uni, too, and it had seemed natural to tell Mr Flemington that was what she went by. Now it felt silly, as if she hadn't grown up yet and couldn't let go of the moniker she'd owned since she'd been small.

"Come in, then." Mrs Flemington stepped back, the sequins glittering.

Rusty glanced inside at the wide hallway, the shiny marble floor, the open-plan layout — a cream lounge to the right, a kitchen and dining area at the back, and to the left, a partial view of the stairs, although what was on the other side was hidden by the front door.

One last chance to go home.

Rusty peered over her shoulder at the deserted street. It wouldn't matter if she turned tail and ran because she didn't know these people, would never have to see them again — they didn't even have her phone number because Mum couldn't afford a line and Rusty had rung Mr Flemington from the corner shop. Just the one evening here wouldn't hurt, would it?

Mum was at the pub, and Rusty would be home by eleven, before her mother. Mr Flemington had said he and his wife were going to dinner and wouldn't be out late. No need for nerves at all.

The money...think of the money.

Rusty stepped inside.

Mrs Flemington closed the door and led the way to the left of the stairs. A door stood ajar closest to her, three others closed farther down. This house appeared much bigger inside than it had from the street. They must have loads of money.

Mrs Flemington knocked on the open door with a knuckle. "Darling, Rusty is here."

"Oh, how delightful!" A head poked out, then a man stepped into the hallway and looked Rusty up and down. He thrust a hand towards her, his tuxedo obviously costing a bomb. "We spoke on the phone. I'm David."

Rusty shook it, feeling all kinds of stupid and out of her depth.

"How remiss of me, and so rude *for not introducing myself earlier," Mrs Flemington trilled. "I'm Valandra."*

Rusty had never heard that name before. Was she Spanish or something? She took the woman's hand, one of Valandra's rings sparkling from the light of a wall-mounted chandelier between two of the doors. The emerald was as big as a penny.

"Let's not chat in my office, too formal. We'll go into the den," David said.

What was a den? The only sort Rusty knew was a secret base at the park.

Rusty followed the couple through the next doorway along. Another living room, although this one was more old-fashioned than the modern one in the open-plan section. The dark-green walls gave it an enclosed air, but Mum would call it cosy. The fireplace, some kind of light wood, had carvings on the side pieces, similar to a totem pole Rusty had seen on the telly. Faces, one on top of the other, the noses pointed, the ends sharp. One had bared shark teeth, another bulging eyes. It was bloody ugly, but she wasn't about to say so—nor would she tell them it gave her the creeps. It was probably one of those family antiques from years ago that was worth thousands.

Brown leather sofas faced each other, a wooden coffee table between, those weird faces on the legs. In the centre, a bowl of potpourri with wisps of something pale between the dried petals and pine cones. It looked like hair but must be some sort of dried grass, gossamer thin.

"Take a seat," David said.

Rusty sat on the edge of a sofa and stared ahead at the wall. Black-and-white photos the likes of which she'd never seen displayed in a home. The images were of body parts—a hand draped over a knee; a close-up of a teary eye; the curve of a backside.

Heat painted Rusty's cheeks.

"Ah, you've spotted my artwork." Valandra perched on the other sofa, careful not to crinkle her dress. "I'm a photographer."

Rusty smiled. She didn't know what to say—her words seemed to have left the building—and she squirmed at being so uncomfortable, not only faced with what could only be described as intimate photos but her lack of confidence when in the company of such a sophisticated couple. She should have babysat for people of her own kind, the ones from her estate who didn't have airs or graces and didn't live in such an extravagant home.

It got her thinking, though, this house, lighting the touchpaper of her dreams—she wanted to have money, to never go hungry again, to swan around in a red sequinned dress, although to be fair, it wasn't her style. She was more of a jeans and T-shirt kind of person. Still, she'd love to have enough cash to afford one.

"Valandra is famous in our circles, you know." David stroked his wife's arm. "She's won awards, and

people from all around want her to take their picture at her studio. We've even had murmurs from royalty, haven't we, darling?"

Rusty smiled, still with no words to offer.

"Anyway, enough of that." Valandra directed her blue-eyed gaze at Rusty. "My husband has had our man look into you—I hope you're not offended, but you can't be too sure of people nowadays, can you."

David chuckled a bit too loudly.

Valandra waited for him to finish. "And he's given us the green light to have you sitting for Anna."

Who was 'our man'? A private detective? A friend? While Rusty understood they wouldn't want any old Tom, Dick, or Harry watching their child, the idea of them poking into who she was left a bad taste in her mouth that seemed to curdle, leaving her thirsty. Had someone followed her? Watched her at home? For the first time, shame at where she lived poked at her. Rendell Street wasn't exactly a good postcode, was it, not like this. At home, kids swore at you rather than be nice, and as for the women... They nattered and sat on their front steps, sequinned dresses so far out of their reach it wasn't funny. The men, rough and ready, either went to the pub after work or sat in front of the telly, a beer can in hand.

"Anna is asleep," David said. "You won't need to do anything but sit and watch television—well, the television in the other lounge. This room is for reading and quiet contemplation—unless, of course, you'd like to read."

"I've brought a book," Rusty said, at last having something she could talk about.

"Excellent!" David beamed. "What's it called?"

Rusty took it out of her bag and showed it to him.

"Theories in Criminology. *Interesting choice.*" David straightened his bow tie. "Is that what you're studying at college?"

"In my free time. I'm going to university in September."

He nodded. "What career choice have you made?"

"I'm interested in law. Being a barrister."

"Good, good. Marvellous for someone like you to aim high. I do believe where we're born doesn't matter, it's what we do with our brain that gets us where we need to be—and what we want. The best-laid plans of mice and men doesn't apply if you're diligent and map things out every step of the way."

Valandra nudged him.

David drummed his fingertips on his knees. "Well, we'd best crack on. Anna won't need tending to at all—don't even bother going upstairs. Once she's asleep, she never wakes, so you're basically earning money for old rope. We could even go out and not have a sitter she's so good at sleeping. She'd have no idea we'd even gone out."

His raucous laughter belted out, startling Rusty.

Valandra tittered and stood. "That would be a terrible thing to do. She's only eight." She stared down at Rusty. "David said you haven't told your mother about doing this job. I hope you won't get into trouble if she finds out. I really couldn't be doing with that kind of negative publicity."

"She...she just worries, that's all," Rusty lied. "And I didn't want twenty questions." Guilt eating away at her from the deception, she wished she'd been honest with Mum, but she really couldn't be doing with the hassle of having her wages stolen and confronting her about it. Best to just earn the money and buy what she needed. Mum might not even notice the new clothes if Rusty didn't show her.

"We all have secrets," Valandra said. "So as long as yours won't come back to bite our bottoms, everything will be fine."

David stood and took his wife's hand. "She's eighteen, darling, she's her own woman. Her mother has no say in what she does." He gave Rusty his attention. "Feel free to make yourself a cup of tea and a sandwich, or whatever you'd like." He winked. "Just don't raid the drinks globe!" He laughed uproariously again. "There's plenty of food in the cupboards, some lovely cakes from the patisserie. We really must dash. Dinner begins at seven."

Rusty clutched her book and followed them into the hallway. Valandra picked a red handbag up from a side table, and they left the house, only the echo of David's weird laugh and their perfume and aftershave lingering behind.

Rusty put her book in her bag and walked over to the kitchen area, staggered by the expensive units and shiny marble worktops. She snooped in wonder—they even had a dishwasher, something unheard of on her estate—and a wine fridge behind one of the cupboard doors. She found a newfangled kettle and made herself a coffee, taking some patisserie cakes out of a cupboard and feeling bad, even though she'd been told to help herself.

She returned to the den, a little off about not checking on Anna, but, paranoid the Flemingtons might have set up nanny cameras, she didn't dare disobey them and go upstairs. On the other sofa—she didn't want the creepy distraction of the photos in front of her—she got on with reading, although she *couldn't concentrate. It must be the unfamiliar surroundings. Maybe next time she'd be more at ease.*

Taking her food and cup, she went to the other lounge and put the telly on. She'd keep the volume low so it didn't disturb Anna.

Maybe she'd get lucky and lose herself in one of the soaps.

Photos on the mantelpiece drew her attention. Two of a little girl, one at each end. Anna. Blonde, pretty, the shots obviously taken by her mother as they were also black and white and done professionally. How weird to be looking after someone she'd never even met.

Rusty shrugged and stuffed a sweet pastry in her mouth.

This was the life.

Later that night, Rusty lay in bed listening to Mum in the next room, shagging some random she'd brought home from the pub. She wished she could leave for university now, but she had a while before her escape route became available. She didn't feel bad for needing to be out of here—she had no compunction to stick around this dead-end place and go nowhere. Like David had said, she needed to use her brain to move

forward in life, and she planned to do that, make something of herself.

Her desire to learn law and become a solicitor or barrister had been with her for a long time. Righting wrongs ranked high on her list, and she looked forward to living in halls and soaking up as much information as she could. Owing student loans was a bugbear she'd have to face when it came time to pay it back, but she was determined to earn enough that she could get rid of them quickly.

She wanted a house filled with nice things like the Flemingtons had, food always in the fridge, wine always on hand. Not that she was a big drinker—how could she be when she saw the effects of alcohol every day? For as long as Rusty could remember, Mum had been unsteady on her feet, and lately, the ravages of booze had grown apparent on her face. Mum had more wrinkles than she should, her eyes bloodshot, her nose red, as if she'd been crying. And maybe she had. Did she think to herself sometimes, that she should have taken a different route? Not been so eager to marry Dad so she could live with him in their little rented house; not take that first sip of vodka which had led to another and another, and instead of sips had turned into bottles; gone to college and trained to be something other than an alcoholic?

What a waste of a life.

The world Rusty lived in had shown her you had to be tough to get where you wanted to be. You had to trample on people to rise to the top. You had to have a singular focus, and nothing could derail it. She'd become a little harder than she'd have liked, cocooning her soft emotions so they weren't on display — so Mum couldn't spot them and use them against her. And Dad, ignoring her like he had, when he only lived a few streets away and she saw him every so often in the corner shop. He'd ensured she had the drive to do better, to be better than him — and the pair of them, Mum and Dad, had shown her that having children wasn't for her. She'd never put a little one through what she'd endured.

A grunted shout from Mum's room meant the bloke had clearly finished what he'd used her for, and Rusty settled on her side, listening to his footsteps thudding on the stairs. Mum would have taken money for the sex, no doubt about it, and, ashamed of her, Rusty closed her eyes.

She'd never let a man treat her like shit.

With the hundred pounds from tonight's babysitting hidden inside a shoe at the bottom of her wardrobe beneath a pile of junk Mum wouldn't think to plough through, Rusty had some of the means to buy the type of clothes that would give people the impression she wasn't from the rough, arse-end of town. She'd be going to Leeds, far enough away from here to put a good distance between her and home. She'd spread her wings, maybe make friends with the other geeks, and see who she really was inside when the manky dressing of her life here had been stripped away. She'd forever be Rusty, or perhaps Coppertop or any other names associated with her hair, but she'd soon get rid of that with dye. She'd reinvent herself, and if she settled in well enough, she wouldn't come home during half term.

Mum needed to learn to stand on her own two feet, to clean up her sick, to fend off the rent man, to run down the off-licence late at night for another bottle of vodka and twenty B&H. It wasn't Rusty's job to do that for much longer, and she couldn't wait to be free.

Chapter Four

Nessa Feathers had a bad feeling in her stomach, the kind you shouldn't ignore. The kind she'd felt many times in her life when it came to her dad. His rants—or warnings, or fatherly advice, as he called them—usually meant she came away from any confrontation with him out of sorts and wishing he'd fall under a bus. At forty, she should have cut him off by now, he brought her nothing but grief, but she believed it was better the devil you know — to keep abreast of what he was up to was better than not being aware. She had her job to protect, and his plans could fuck it up for her. But maybe he wouldn't last much longer. He smoked too many cigars and drank too much lager and brandy, on his way to killing himself with years of bad health choices. Nessa didn't think she'd get that lucky in her dad snuffing it. He'd probably live until he was ninety knowing her luck.

The reason for her sore stomach jumped into her head again. George had been unusually rude, and she worried he'd found out what Dad was up to. That was the trouble with George and Greg, they sometimes let people think they didn't know what was going on, pouncing later, catching them red-handed. Fucking hell. But why take it out on her by being grumpy? Oh God, did he know *she* knew?

Hmm, but he'd apologised, so that didn't add up. Unless he realised he'd let his mask slip and didn't want her twigging so had said sorry to cover it up.

She should have said something to George long before now. At first, she'd thought Dad had been pulling her leg to see her reaction, toying with her so she thought her job here was in jeopardy if he got caught—he loved to see her face drop when he said mean things. But it had soon become clear that he was deadly serious. He still had contacts in the game, but the goalposts had changed so much since he'd been in his heyday that she wasn't sure he could trust the people he'd be selling the stolen goods to. The buyers would probably be the new breed of gangland, and they worked differently. They'd see him as an old duffer, maybe bugger off without paying. Or shoot him in the head so there was no trace back to them buying nicked shit.

She should find out who they were.

And who had he roped in to do it with him other than his best mate, Jordy? He'd mentioned a team of men—what, were all the elderly ex-Cardigan employees banding together for one last hurrah? She'd laugh, but it wasn't funny.

Nessa left the bar in the capable hands of the staff and rounded the counter to go and see her father. She didn't want to go anywhere near him, but she had to protect herself and what she'd achieved here, so finding out more was her aim. For the first time in her life, she was proud of her position. She wasn't just a barmaid anymore, someone to be spoken to like a piece of shit. She *managed* this place, loved it to death, and couldn't allow Dad to have it taken away from her.

She nodded to people as she passed, stopping to enquire whether they were happy with their meals and the service. She was good at front-of-house duties, had "the banter" as Mum said.

She grimaced at thoughts of her mother, a woman who'd never bonded with Nessa in the way she should have. Married to a man who ruled the roost, Beverly Feathers was a shadow of the woman she must have been when she'd met her husband. Years of beating browbeaten had crushed her spirit and dulled the sparkle in her eyes. Nessa knew how that felt. Dad tried to intimidate her all the time. It had worked years ago, but these days she saw him for who he was. A nasty prick.

According to the stories, ones he dredged up so he could boast, he'd been a hard bastard in his day. He could still give someone a run for their money in the verbal stakes if he had to, but he'd gone to fat recently—too many free meals here. If the twins found out he didn't pay for them, she'd be out on her arse. But he still relied on his notoriety to bully Mum, and rather than feel sorry for her, Nessa wished she'd grow some balls and bite back at him like she'd learned to.

He sat in a booth with one of his cronies from back in the day, the bloke he used to go around with when they'd worked for Ron Cardigan. Jordy Robinson, an overweight, craggy-faced former bruiser with wet, rubbery lips, raised his grey eyebrows at her in silent question, probably because she hadn't brought free pints with her. He was a right skinflint and got on her nerves for not putting his hand in his pocket. She didn't like the way he looked at her, never had. Pervert.

She ignored him and sat beside her father, checking for people earwigging. One last attempt to get him to pack this in, and if he didn't listen, he was up shit creek, she'd make sure of it. She'd direct his fate, and he could suffer the consequences.

Leaning in, she said quietly, "George had a major cob on with me when he was in. Do you think he knows?"

Dad laughed, a hand to his chest, his flabby belly jiggling. His dentures came loose, and he snapped them back in place, cheeks reddening. He didn't like people knowing he'd succumbed to old age by having false teeth. He'd had a gold one put in the front, said it made him look hard.

Twat.

He calmed down. "I doubt it. We'd be dead by now if he did, and it's been a while since we heard him and Greg talking in here about the stash—no way would they keep it quiet for this long if they knew what we were up to. Anyway, it serves them right for speaking loudly. Who could blame us for running with that kind of information? They handed it to us on a plate. You'd think they'd know better. You wouldn't see Ron discussing business in front of the public."

Nessa didn't agree with 'serves them right'. The twins had been good to her, paid her well, had given her the flat upstairs, and they didn't deserve to be fucked over.

Dad and Jordy weren't young anymore, their brains didn't fire on all cylinders, not enough for them to pull off such a stunt anyway. It was dangerous, fucking with The Brothers, and while she was hacked off that George had barked at her, she didn't want to see one of their businesses turned over. The fallout didn't bear thinking about. She wouldn't have a father anymore, that much was certain (not a bad thing, mind). Nessa had tried to talk Dad and Jordy out of it a few times already, but they were adamant. She couldn't imagine them successfully pulling off a raid nowadays, old codgers that they were, but it seemed they thought differently.

"What if someone heard you two talking about it?" she asked. "They could have gone and told them. Do you trust the others you've brought in on this? What if they've blabbed? What about the buyers? Can you trust *them*? And the hairdresser's might be like Fort Knox now. I heard they were going to open with a soft launch a couple of weeks ago then didn't bother. They opened today, my mate went and got her barnet done, but what if they took the past two weeks to secure the place to such a degree that you'll never get in because they *know you're coming*? It's all very well using a battering ram like you said, but what if the doors are steel like they are here?"

Dad bristled and gave her a filthy look. "We've had our ears to the ground, someone watching. Nothing's been done since it was first renovated, so don't worry your ugly little head about it."

Ugly little head. She examined her feelings on that and found it didn't hurt. Not anymore.

"We're going in tonight," he said. "It's all sorted."

Oh God, so soon? "Are you *sure* you've thought it all through? Those windows, you can bet they're bulletproof, so if the doors don't bust in, that glass won't either."

Dad eyed her. "What's your fucking game, kid? Why are you questioning me? You think you're all that and a bag of chips now you run this place. You wouldn't have got the fucking job if it wasn't for me putting a good word in." He gestured at their surroundings. "People like you are two a penny. You're easily replaceable, don't forget that."

This wasn't the first time Dad had threatened her. As a kid, she'd regularly been on the other end of his dished-out warnings, as if she didn't matter, like she was the same as everyone else — if she got in his way, he'd mow her down.

Jordy nudged him. "Did you just warn your daughter you'd take her out? You'd *kill* her? I didn't have you down for *that* much of a cunt, mate."

Dad shrugged. "Take it how you want. Nessa knows which side her bread's buttered."

"That's out of order," Jordy said. "There's something wrong with you up top. You don't turn on family." He sniffed. "You can go off people, you know."

"Fuck off," Dad grumbled. "I was letting her know that just as easily as she got this job, she could lose it. No one likes a Betty Bragger, and she's been blowing her own trumpet a lot lately. If the twins think she's got too big for her boots, she'll be out on her ear."

Nessa sat back, shame driving through her. Shame that her father was such a dick and spoke to people that way. He'd never seen her as anything but a burden—because she wasn't a son. His disappointment that Mum hadn't given him one had been thrust in Nessa's face for as long as she could remember. By God, she didn't like him, never really had. She wasn't aware she'd been bragging, so him saying that was a bit of a shock. Was that how it came across to everyone, or had he just said that to take her down a peg? To dim her shine?

"She's got a right to be happy she's landed on her feet," Jordy said. "*Years* she's been working in dead-end jobs. Leave her alone."

Nessa wasn't green. She was well aware Jordy was only sticking up for her so much because he wanted another free pint, although to be fair, he *had* fought her corner before, so she shouldn't be so harsh. Then she remembered his leers and changed her mind on being grateful to him.

"Don't say I didn't warn you." She stood and returned to the bar, pouring Jordy a lager and taking it over to make a point.

He grinned at her. "Cheers, darlin'. You're a diamond."

"Oi, where's mine?" Dad growled.

She shoved a hand on her hip. "Oh, maybe you might want to go and ask one of the bar staff to pour you one, seeing as I'm so shit at my job. I mean, I might spill it I'm so useless."

She flounced off, her anger towards him coiling into a knot in her stomach. She fucking *hated* him and wished he'd got gunned down years ago. Wished Ron had done it.

Behind the bar, she slapped on a smile, conscious she was playing the part of manager in an over-the-top way to prove to Dad she wasn't hurt by what he'd said. She wasn't young anymore, someone easily intimidated, for fuck's sake. What he thought of her didn't matter. She wanted to teach him a lesson. Show him he wasn't a bag of chips himself. Fucking prick.

She served customers, ignoring him when he came up to the bar, leaving someone else to serve him, which forced him to pay. She thought about her childhood and how shitty she'd felt because of her parents. Mum was a wet lettuce, letting Dad say whatever he liked to her and Nessa. The pair of them should never have had children. *She* didn't want any, too afraid that their ways would rub off on her parenting, his snide comments creeping in when she spoke to her child.

Sorry for the little girl she'd been, she served pint after pint, her jaw aching she smiled so much. Dad slouched off ten minutes later, Jordy right behind him. They'd probably go to their lock-up where they stored hooky gear and get ready to do the raid. Who did he think he was, taking on The Brothers?

A massive wave of resentment took over her, and she stormed into her office and locked the door. Sat at the desk with her forehead in her hands. She'd definitely tell the twins. If she didn't and lost this job—or worse, they kneecapped her if they found out she'd known about this and hadn't said—she'd become an outcast around here. No one would be pleased to see her like they were in the Noodle. She had mini celebrity status, sort of, as if she trod the boards on her own stage and the audience lapped up her performance.

She *was* good at her job. She bloody was.

And she was also good at getting her own back for years of being emotionally and mentally crucified.

Chapter Five

George parked the BMW in the garage and entered the house via the connecting door that led to the kitchen. He placed the takeaway bag on the worktop. The room looked exactly the same as when he'd left it, no Greg cooking lunch earlier and stacking his plate in the dishwasher, no coffee cups soaking in the sink. He wandered into the lounge and found the same again—a spotless room. What he wouldn't give for his brother's jacket to be draped over a chair or his red tie slung over a cushion.

He sighed and walked upstairs, his steps weary. He had to hand it to Moon et al—running an estate on your own was harder than he'd thought, and he was knackered. All right, he'd had an easier day today, looking after Harper instead of running around, but lethargy still weighed down his muscles. He now had more respect for mothers who coped with children by themselves. That baby had some serious energy, and George had to keep his wits about him to make sure Harper didn't do himself a mischief, crawling all over the place.

He took a deep breath and went into Greg's room. Last week, going in there had been torture, seeing the bed made, his brother not in it. George had put away some washing, crying when hanging Greg's ironed shirts, guilt that he'd allowed his twin to get shot soaking into his bones yet again. He'd promised to protect him always and had failed. The tears had turned into self-hatred, although Moon had reminded him that they'd *all* walked into that abattoir fridge, knowing they could be shot—Greg had a mind of his own and could have refused to go in. But it was what they did, striding into danger, and because neither of them had been injured before, they'd become complacent.

Or I had.

A bullet had skimmed George's ear—fuck, it had hurt—but it was nothing compared to Greg taking a bullet to his chest. George's graze had scabbed over and was well on the way to being healed, but it still burned every so often, as if reminding him of what had happened.

To vent his rage, George had obliterated Mrs Whitehall, a leader who'd ordered her men to shoot them. The leader meeting that had followed, where he'd had to explain his actions… Thank God he'd had Moon, Tick-Tock, and Lincoln as witnesses to back him up. Whitehall's death had been classed as justified, and with Lincoln providing information from planting one of his men in Whitehall's camp, proof that she'd been a dodgy cow who should never have run an estate, the case had been closed. Lincoln had taken over her estate, and Moon, albeit unhappy about it at first, had stepped in to man a large patch that had once been two manors—Golden Eye and Judas, seeing as Prince, another iffy leader, had been dealt with as well. Moon had renamed the lot to match his own area, using his best men, Brickhouse and Alien, to help run it.

"All right, cockwomble?" Greg looked relieved to have some company.

George smiled. "Not too bad, bruv. You'd better not have got up and gone downstairs today, being sneaky and pretending you've been in bed all this time." He sat on the bottom of the mattress.

"Nah. I'm bored off my tits, though."

"Tough, the clinic said you need to rest for a month before you get back on the horse."

"That's bullshit." Greg gestured to the wheeled table George had bought. "And *that* only makes me feel like I'm in hospital, an invalid."

A mini fridge sat on top, the six cans of Coke that had been in it this morning empty beside it. Next to that, a plate with balled-up clingfilm on it and a splodge of piccalilli—those bloody disgusting sandwiches George made him every morning for lunch. In short, he ensured his brother had all the food he needed so he didn't have to get up and make it himself. He was allowed to the bathroom, but that was it. In a private conversation out of Greg's earshot, the doctor at the clinic *had* said Greg would benefit from short walks around the house, but George had chosen not to tell him that. He didn't like keeping secrets, but he'd worried about the stitches bursting.

And you wanted to mollycoddle him again.

The bullet had lodged inside Greg, he hadn't got lucky with a through-and-through. He'd died on that steel table at the abattoir. George had felt it in his soul the moment his twin had slipped away, and he'd screamed at the ceiling, *feeling* his other half being ripped from him. Lincoln had brought Greg back to life after an agonisingly long time, and they'd rushed him to the private clinic. George, Moon, and Tick-Tock had stayed while Greg's operation had taken place, George pacing, getting on their nerves. In the end, not knowing whether Greg would die again in theatre, he'd had to do something to stop himself from imploding. Do what Greg would have wanted: go and see what was up with Faith Lemon.

A week in the clinic, and Greg had come home, George pandering to him, Greg calling him a fanny. George had returned to work, hating leaving Greg but having to maintain the façade that everything was all right. He'd held off telling anyone but Anna about the shooting because one, he couldn't handle saying it out loud, and two, Greg didn't want anyone knowing. Two more weeks of this, then they could run the estate together again.

"I bought you a carbonara from the Noodle if you're hungry," George said.

"Cheers."

"What have you been up to?"

"Watching bollocks on telly and slowly going mental. You?"

George told him about Anna. "So it got me thinking that just because someone doesn't look like they've been through that sort of crap, I shouldn't dismiss it when we hear about these stories from Mason or Janine."

Greg tutted. "*We* shouldn't dismiss it. We both assumed Anna was one of the other Anna Barkers—boring life, nothing to write home about. Stop putting everything on your shoulders. Like me being shot. It was inevitable one of us would cop a bullet at some point. We'd been lucky before that not to be hurt. *I* chose to walk into that fridge just like you did. *I* took the risk. You've got to stop being my protector. Cut yourself some slack, for fuck's sake. We're not five anymore. There's no Richard to save me from."

For as far back as George could remember, he'd protected Greg. From Richard, their so-called father, from bullies at school, from everything. It was a part of his makeup, something he did subconsciously, naturally, and now, because of what had happened, he'd be even worse. He'd pampered him since he'd come home from the clinic, a clucking hen, so relieved Greg lived and breathed, and while it obviously got on Greg's nellies, George had carried on regardless.

He sighed. "You're my everything. I've got to make sure you're okay. I never want to go through that again. I don't want *you* going through it."

"Then we'll have to give up the estate, because we're going to get hurt again at some point. Face it, we do a nasty job. You can't cover my arse all the time. I know why you insist we stick together when we're out there, so you can watch out for me, but how do you think I feel when you fuck off as Ruffian and leave me on my own? *I* worry about *you*, too. *I* want to protect *you*. I want to make up for all the times you took the wallops when we were kids—to be there for you instead of the other way round. I'm glad it was me who got shot. Glad it was me who took the pain for once, because you've been doing that for me my whole life. It was about time it was me."

George digested that. It tasted bitter, but he'd accept it. "Fine. I won't hover round you like a blue-arsed fly, but I'll be watching, always making sure you're okay. Bulletproof vest now, every day, no matter what we're doing."

"Shall we wear helmets an' all? We could get shot in the head."

George glared at him. "Don't be sarky, you dick."

Greg laughed. "So what's happening about this Bastard bloke?"

"Janine's looking into him. I've gotta say, working without you is…shit."

"Right." Greg threw the quilt off and swung his legs out of bed.

"What do you think *you're* doing?" George frowned.

"Getting up, what's it look like?"

"Lie back down, you prick. You might hurt yourself."

Greg flicked George's nose. "Fuck off. I've been going to the bathroom and back all right, I'm not winded, so I'm coming back to work."

"No you're not."

Greg stood. Pointed. "That's enough now. Pack it in—I didn't die…for long. I'm still here, pissing you off. You can do all the hard work, I'll just tag along and point out where you're going wrong, like usual."

"Never thought I'd miss that, you getting on my wick." George smiled. "I cry on and off, you know. Can't get it out of my head."

Greg blinked. "Don't. The thought of you blubbing…" He took a shuddering breath. "We'll be more careful. Take better precautions. Think before we act—which is what *I* try to do, but you're always gung-ho. That's got to stop."

"Noted."

Greg knuckled an eye. "We'll be all right, bruv."

George nodded. "We'd better be."

Chapter Six

*L*ast night, as Rusty had left the Flemingtons'
home, David had asked her to babysit again the
next evening. Valandra had some function or other at
her studio, selling large prints of her photos, and
they'd be gone until the early hours as, "These things
tend to go on and on, people drunk as lords." He'd
suggested Rusty stay over—they'd pay her five
hundred pounds because of the responsibility and

inconvenience—and they'd be home in time for when Anna woke up, around six a.m.

Rusty couldn't believe her luck. All that money just for sitting there reading or watching telly? For sleeping? She'd only planned to earn three hundred quid, but already the cash was becoming addictive. Imagine what she could make if she carried on between now and going to uni?

The couple had left in a flurry of excitement, and Rusty went into the den. One of the sofas was the pull-out kind, and a bed had been made up for her. A white broderie anglaise quilt cover draped to the floor, and scatter cushions in different greens—to match the walls, she reckoned—gave it a stately feel. She'd dreamed of sleeping in a posh bed like this, especially one with a proper velvet blanket the colour of Valandra's ring at the bottom.

She placed her bag on the coffee table, which had been moved in front of the bay window, and took out her nightie and slippers. David had said she could use the downstairs bathroom to save her going upstairs and potentially waking Anna by mistake.

Washbag in hand, she followed the directions he'd given her and walked next door into the poshest bathroom she'd ever seen. Golden taps in the black-tiled shower cubicle and the two sinks beside the toilet.

Pure-white towels with black ribbon trim on a free-standing rail. Small soaps displayed in a pretty basket, along with shampoo and conditioner, toothpaste, even a toothbrush in its packet. Maybe they had people who came to stay often, although she doubted they'd be relegated to a sofa bed. They'd have one of the rooms upstairs.

Still, it was all better than at home—no mould in the corners for a start—and she wouldn't look a gift horse in the mouth. She managed to work out how to switch on the shower and chose some of the toiletries. Taking her clothes off, she folded them on the vanity between the sinks and stepped under the spray.

She could get used to this.

She woke with a start. Was that a scream, short, sharp, but over quickly? She recalled her dream—being chased by a monster—so had she been the one screaming? For a moment, she couldn't recall where she was, then the sight of that crying eye in one of the pictures, lit up by a nearby lamp, reminded her. She shot out of bed and into the hallway, her heart rate sky-high, her legs going weak. What if someone had got into the house? She had to make sure Anna was okay.

Valandra stood at the bottom of the stairs, clutching the front of her black silk gown, a tendril of hair slipping from the elaborate bun on the top of her head. Even then she still looked elegant. David flew down the stairs, his face red, his eyes showing how frantic he was.

"She's not in any of the bedrooms," he said, panting.

"What?" Valandra shrieked. "She must be! She isn't down here either. Oh God, my baby…"

Rusty tried to catch up to what was going on, her mind still thick with sleep. "What's…what's happened?"

"Anna's gone," Valandra wailed and sank onto the bottom step.

"We'll have to phone the police," David said. "Did you notice if the back door had been tampered with, darling?"

Valandra rubbed her forehead. "No, it's still locked."

David lunged at Rusty and held her upper arms. He shook her. "Did you hear anything? Someone coming in?"

She swallowed her fear at the darkness in his eyes. "No! I went to bed at ten and only just woke up."

"The cellar," Valandra said. "Maybe she went down there to play a trick on Rusty. I told Anna she was coming—she could have woken up and…and…"

David let Rusty go. He rushed to the door at the far end on the left, past his office, the den, and the bathroom. He stared at the key in the lock. "She had to have come down here. That key's usually in the pot by the front door."

"Oh, thank God, the little devil." Valandra kicked her heels off and went over to him. "Come with us," she said to Rusty. "Just in case there is an intruder. I don't want to leave you in case we disturb him and he comes running up here."

Terror thudded through Rusty. She wanted to go home, not stay here, but she felt responsible for Anna going missing, even though she'd been told to not go upstairs and check on her. The idea of some man breaking in brought on a shiver, but she walked to the door and waited for David to open it.

"Anna?" he called into the void. "Are you down there?"

"Daddy!" Faint, reedy.

"Are you all right?"

"I've got my foot stuck."

David's face registered his relief, and he looked at his wife, tears filling her eyes. "We really need to have a chat with her about playing tricks. This one has gone too far. I thought she'd been kidnapped, for goodness sake."

Valandra smiled at Rusty. "I'm so sorry about this. Anna's such a minx. This is why we have to give her special medicine to keep her asleep at night so we at least get some respite."

Alarm surged through Rusty.

"Oh no," Valandra said, "don't look so panicked. The doctor gave it to us on prescription."

Relieved a little by that, although drugging a child wasn't on her list of RIGHT THINGS TO DO, Rusty smiled back, her lips wobbling. "I should go home now. She's been found so…"

"Nonsense," David said. "Come and meet her."

A squeal from down below ripped upstairs. "Daddy, there's a big spider."

"Hang on, cherub."

David disappeared into the black doorway, his footsteps tapping, getting fainter as he must be going down some stairs. Valandra flicked a light switch just inside the frame. Pale illumination flooded the white-painted wall, confusing Rusty for a moment. She'd expected breeze blocks or bricks, seeing as it led to a cellar, a few cobwebs as decoration, but maybe it *wasn't the scary, dank place she'd imagined and more of an extra living space.*

"I'm so terribly sorry about Anna," Valandra said. "She's what you might call...difficult to handle. She gets bored easily, you see, and tends to get up to mischief. Her medicine must have worn off." She glanced at her delicate wristwatch. "Oh, it is five-fifteen, so I suppose I shouldn't complain..."

She disappeared into the doorway.

Rusty didn't want to meet a child who could shit people up so easily. She supposed they hadn't told her about Anna's behaviour because she was so doped up while sleeping, Rusty would never encounter it. If the girl liked playing these kinds of jokes, it was a wonder David and Valandra didn't appear more frazzled. They always seemed so put-together, poised, charming. Was that the same front Rusty put on each day because of her unstable mother, to mask what was really going on behind closed doors? Did rich people have crosses to bear, too?

She moved to the doorway and stared ahead. Another doorway with a keyhole. For storage? She looked left. Just a normal stairway, the steps varnished wood, the black iron handrails thick and chunky, scrolls on the ends nearest to her. At the bottom, a small patch of landing, carpeted in royal blue, so yes, more living space.

Rusty walked down and reached the last step. She turned to peer to her left—a wall at the end of the short landing, another of Valandra's photos on it, this time a foot with dark polish on the nails. More steps, again to the left, but only three. It made sense, as they'd lead to the underside of the house. She crept along, the sound of David soothing Anna floating up to her, Valandra saying she'd dispose of the spider in the toilet.

They had a toilet *down there?*

At the bottom of the second set of stairs, a door on the right, ajar. A toilet flushed, and Valandra swanned across the gap, her bare feet slapping on shiny floorboards. Rusty poked the door with a finger to open it wider, then popped her head around.

"Oh, here she is, Anna Doll," David said.

Rusty took in the space first—a studio flat, around the same size as the open-plan area above. David and Anna sat on a black leather corner sofa placed in the centre farthest away, a kitchenette cordoned off by one of the sofa sides, a slightly open door at the end of a row of cupboards that clearly led to a bedroom—a built-in wardrobe stood in view. Rusty estimated the bedroom was beneath the dining area. She glanced over to where

Valandra had come from—a bathroom, much like the one she'd used earlier, all black tiles and gold taps.

Then she stared at Anna.

In pink Barbie pyjamas, the girl appeared afraid, her damp eyes pleading with Rusty for…for what? Or was she still spooked by her encounter with the spider? The place was so clean, Rusty couldn't imagine how a spider had even got in. Anna lowered her eyes and fiddled with her fingers in her lap, her bottom lip sticking out.

"What do you say for scaring Rusty?" David asked.

"Sorry," Anna said.

"Right, let's get you some breakfast." He stood, scooped her into his arms, and breezed past Rusty.

She turned to watch them go.

Anna stared at her over David's shoulder and mouthed, "Run!"

What? A glut of fear pounded through Rusty, and she made it out of the door to leg it upstairs.

"Do you like the flat?" Valandra asked, stalling her with a hand on her arm.

Rusty spun round to find the woman standing a bit too close, the scent of her strong perfume wafting up her nose. "Um, yes, it's nice."

"Come and have a better look."

"No, I should go really. I…"

Valandra held Rusty's wrist and guided her inside, closing the door.

"It belonged to David's mother once upon a time," *she said as if Rusty hadn't spoken. "She had him in her late forties, so of course, by the time he grew up, she was pretty infirm. She wet the bed, kept falling over, needed feeding, which was ghastly. We kept her down here out of the way. She was a dreadful sight at one point."*

Out of the way? What the hell?

"David beat the shit out of her. The bruises were quite hideous."

Rusty eyed the woman for signs that she was joking, but there were none. She reached back for the door handle. People who hurt old ladies...she didn't want anything to do with them. Then there was drugging Anna. Should she go to the police? Where was his mother now? Dead? Was this why Anna had told her to run?

A click echoed behind her.

Valandra smiled. "That will be David, locking us in. Please, do take a seat." She held a hand out towards the sofa. This time, a ruby ring glinted in the light.

Rusty yanked at the handle. It went down, but the door wouldn't open. Panic spun a wicked web inside her, and she tugged and shouted, tears falling, a lump crashing into her throat.

"It's pointless," Valandra said. "No one gets out of here alive. Now then, come and sit with me so I can explain the rules."

Rules?

Rusty banged on the door with the sides of her fists—what Valandra had said implied Rusty would die here.

Not if she had anything to do with it.

"No one will hear you. Do you think we'd be so stupid as to allow people to listen to your screams? And you *will* scream."

Rusty kicked the door, but it didn't break like the thin wooden one at home had when Mum had thumped it that time.

"They're steel behind the wood." Valandra sighed. "And as you'd see if you bothered to stop being so silly, all the windows have been bricked up to the ceilings. Only the tops of them can be seen from outside, and they've been painted white, so no one will spot you from there. The flat is soundproofed. You're ours now, Rusty, although I do feel we need another nickname. I did tell you I liked them."

Rusty stopped kicking, her forehead falling against the door. She breathed deeply, trying to get her *thoughts in order. They'd locked her in this flat. No one knew where she was. No one would hear her scream.*

Fuck. Fuck!

"Slave, that's it," Valandra said. *"That suits you nicely."*

Chapter Seven

Two hours after seeing George, Janine sat at her desk and refreshed her email. Earlier, a warrant had been granted for her to access the man in question's bank account and any credit cards, her excuse that she was concerned about a possible threat to life and she needed to track his movements. This meant she'd have to play this by the book, alerting her DCI in the morning that

Anna had been paid a visit. The fact the man would 'disappear' would be put down to the case going cold, that after his initial appearance today, he hadn't bothered Anna again so Janine hadn't felt the need to chase it up.

She'd contacted the bank—an online-only one—and they'd sent the PDF statements through. Although she'd made out to George that she might get into trouble for snooping, she wouldn't on this occasion. She often looked up this case as a part of her job. It had disturbed her from the start, back when she'd been in her teens, and the DCI knew of her interest. Over the years, she'd used it as a study when taking new officers under her wing, teaching them that although a family may *look* decent and law-abiding on the outside, behind closed doors, monsters lurked. Those who she'd taught now understood to peer far beyond the first impression, to ask themselves: *Are they* really *on the level?* And to trust the very real gut instinct, an inbuilt radar that warned you something wasn't right, because ignoring it could get you in a whole heap of shit. Janine did it all the time, assessing those she came into contact with in her duties, and had even done it with George and Greg.

Stare behind the mask, always.

So familiar with the information, she didn't need to read the file again, but she *did* need to check when Bastard—a good name, and one she'd adopt when thinking of him—had been released. She hadn't checked for a while. Life had been busy, no time to delve for an idle nose, and since Colin, her DS, the most recent addition to the team, hadn't needed any lessons in how to look beyond the veil when he'd been assigned to be her sergeant, she hadn't accessed the file to show him.

Bastard had been let out eighteen months ago. Paroled for six months and living in a bedsit, a far cry from what he'd been used to before he'd been nicked. He'd existed on benefits and likely any savings he'd stashed away prior to being caught for his crimes. Why did he think Anna would want to reconnect with him? George had said he'd approached her in Manchester the first time, where she'd lived, and Anna had run away, which made it clear she didn't want to know. Why push it, then, by finding out she'd come to London? Why follow her here and look for her? What was his agenda?

Janine recalled certain aspects of the case, and her blood ran cold. Surely he didn't... No, he wouldn't want to start up his antics again involving Anna. That would be sick—and while he *was* sick, she didn't think he'd stoop to that level. The thought that he'd even been let out was a joke—that man was still a danger to society, a menace, and he needed to be taken out of the equation permanently.

Janine had long since accepted that straddling the line between good copper and bad might get her into hot water, but sometimes, the brand of justice the leaders used got the *correct* job done—some people didn't deserve to go to prison when their victims were dead, they needed to die, too. She should abhor breaking the law—she'd vowed to uphold it, not encourage people to commit crimes—but her strong sense of getting fitting justice overrode that. Her past dictated her present and always would. What she'd seen in her lifetime meant she wanted people dead, not lounging around in the nick.

In this particular case, she'd like nothing more than to see Bastard six feet under, and she'd help the twins to do it, even watch while they sawed him up. Maybe she could speak to Anna afterwards, put her mind at rest that no one would come for her and she could live her life free of worry at last.

She looked through his financials more intently. He'd opened the bank account after leaving prison, transferring funds from NatWest, likely the previous bank he'd used. A thousand had gone out to a Peter Warson—she'd look him up in a minute. Benefits had been paid into it ever since, and he was a minimal-spend kind of person for several months after being a free man. He never spent more than his benefits, his transferred savings intact apart from that grand.

She paused for a moment at the sight of him using the card in a nightclub at Albion Wharf, Manchester—the night he'd approached Anna. From there, nothing of import had occurred, until he'd paid Warson again, five hundred this time. Then he'd bought a rail ticket to London last month. Rent payments had switched to his current address—a shitty little street she knew well.

Interesting.

What if he planned to do something to Anna? Take her off and hide her? It would make sense, considering she'd basically been hidden from the world before. Maybe he wanted to hide her again. He'd undoubtedly think she wouldn't want to tell anyone she'd seen him because she likely carried a sense of shame with her about her past and she'd want it kept a secret. Had Anna not told George about this, Bastard could well have done whatever it was he'd come to do, and it would appear, if that was his intention, that she'd just gone missing.

But what if he only wanted to talk to her, clear a few things up? Beg for her forgiveness? It wasn't unheard of for people who'd spent time in prison to abruptly realise the error of their ways at the first clang of their cell door shutting. He'd had a while to contemplate his actions. Perhaps 'sorry' was all he wanted to say.

She scanned the account further. After staring at Anna earlier, he'd gone to a nearby McDonald's, then the cinema, then a visit to an ice cream place that sold waffles and the like. A simple evening out for a man who hadn't had the pleasure of doing something like that for a while. On his income, he'd need to be careful with his spending habits if he kept this up. His benefits were meagre. Or wasn't he worried about that now? Did he intend to worm his way into Anna's affections and mooch off her?

Or was this a celebratory treat?

The idea of that had her feeling sick.

Janine closed the last PDF and brought up the police database. She typed in *Peter Warson*, getting several hits. But only one lived in Manchester. She switched to Google and put the name in again. At the top was a Peter Warson, private detective—he'd clearly paid for his business to be the first on the list.

So that's how he found Anna.

She shut her computer down. She had Bastard's address, so she'd pass it on to George but also go and have a gander for herself. She had to, considering she'd asked for that warrant; she'd see this through as though it was an active investigation.

She left the station and drove away, spotting Cameron's car in her rearview. Comforted by his continual presence, something she hadn't wanted at first but had got used to—*and* him living in her house—she smiled at what George had said. They *had* been kissing, and she worried where this was going, whether she could handle opening herself up to a man. She'd sworn off them for life. Told herself she didn't need anyone but herself. She hadn't exactly had good role models of the male variety, her father a loser, other pricks presenting as complete and utter arseholes, only out for themselves. George and Greg—and Cameron—were the only exceptions in her book: good, decent people, even if they *did* incite bloodshed and break a thousand laws.

She'd found herself warming to Cameron ever since he'd walked into her house and announced he had cameras to put up so the twins could keep an eye on whether anyone broke in to kill her. Although she fancied him, she'd kept her feelings to herself, but over time, he'd crept into her affections, and recently, she'd begun to think about a life without him in it. When everyone from The Network had been rounded up and she was safe, he'd leave.

And she didn't want him to.

Never thought I'd hear myself saying that.

She arrived at the address and parked, staring at the large shared house. Lights on in two bay windows, one on top of the other, none on the highest floor where he lived. She had reason to go and knock on the door, ask him why he'd acted suspiciously at Under the Dryer today—maybe that would be enough to stop him from going back. It was what the DCI would expect her to do. But why should she alert Bastard that someone was onto him? Better that he remained oblivious until the twins turned up. Over the next couple of days, she'd make out to her boss she'd been here a few times and no one had answered. Give George and Greg time to nab him.

On her burner, she texted them, passed on what she'd found out. What they did with his address was their business. So long as they alerted her when Bastard had been apprehended, she could then inform the DCI that he seemed to be in the wind and hadn't approached Anna again.

She didn't like her job overlapping her secret life with The Brothers, but on this occasion, it had been necessary. The warrant, contacting the bank—she couldn't have done it legitimately otherwise.

GG: CHEERS. WE'LL SEND ICHABOD TO WATCH HIS COMINGS AND GOINGS FOR A BIT, THEN MAKE OUR MOVE.

She sighed and drove off, wondering what Anna was like. Had she turned out okay? It was difficult not to speculate, considering Janine was so close to the intricacies of the case. She'd often thought about her. If she'd have opened the file more recently, she'd have been aware Anna had come to London. What would Janine have done with that information, though? It wasn't like she could turn up on her doorstep, introduce herself, and ask questions. She doubted she'd be welcome. And admitting that she was au fait with every aspect of what had gone on might make her look like a weirdo, despite being a police officer. After all, Anna likely didn't trust the police.

And who the fuck could blame her?

Chapter Eight

He sat in his room in the dark, thinking about Anna. She'd filled his thoughts while he'd been in prison, her laughter trilling inside his head. He could still see every aspect of his past as if fresh, and, eyes closed on his bunk, the air musty from the stale sweat of his cellmate, he'd walked through its halls, a ghost inspecting the imprints left behind of everything he'd done and said, as if actions and words were tangible things, hanging around, sentimental trinkets he could touch and feel. Many an occasion he'd indulged himself in watching scenes as he'd seen them the first time round, subtle differences springing out at him, ones he'd failed to pick up on before. How awful he looked, what a dreadful person he'd have been perceived as. But at the time it had been normal and, the two sides of his life butting against each other, he'd tiptoed a dodgy road.

Therapists and the priest in HMP Belmarsh had been willing to save him, or had a good go trying. He knew all the tricks and so answered according to what they wanted to hear. His time in the nick had been less fraught than it could have been, him becoming the golden child as it were, the one prisoner who could redeem himself. Those who expressed a fondness to repent were treated differently, protected by the screws. He'd pretended to find a love of God, although it was only that, pretending, but his deception had served its purpose, and he'd been seen as less of an instigator and more of a sad victim.

Lies could get you where you wanted to be, and he'd used them to his advantage without remorse. Everyone wielded their own paintbrush with which they could create a picture the viewer took at face value. The brushstrokes may be added to the canvas with malice but the emotion remained unseen—a brushstroke appeared as a brushstroke after all, nothing more. But the image he'd created had been the shield he'd hidden behind, a way to get through his days unscathed. Not at the beginning, though. *Those* days had been awful. He'd been given the label of someone the other inmates detested, and he'd been beaten, bitten, raped, treated as nothing but a punchbag.

They had no idea it had turned him on.

He switched his mind away from the vulgarities of incarceration and back to Anna, how he'd viewed her today. She'd changed from that time in Manchester. No longer ravaged by booze and hard living, she'd appeared fresh-faced and happy. He wanted to keep her safe—her being out in the open like that, where anyone could snatch her away and kill her, wasn't something he could handle. While locked inside, he'd made a promise to himself to protect her as soon as he could, and when he'd left prison, he'd set about finding her. As he'd been in Belmarsh, considered a threat to the public—bloody ridiculous—he'd expected Anna to still be in the same vicinity, but Warson had informed him she'd moved to Manchester shortly after it had all kicked off.

He'd waited out his six months' parole, behaved as well as he had in prison, where he'd convinced everyone who mattered he was no longer a danger, then he'd headed north, free to do so without having to check in with a nosy-beak officer. Warson had passed on her address. There followed a few weeks of tailing her, until he'd finally walked up behind her and introduced himself.

That she'd spurned him, had stared at him, horrified, then run away… It had *hurt*. Didn't she understand he loved her? Wanted to take care of her? That she belonged with him?

He'd haunted her favourite drinking spots for a while before he'd twigged she'd done a runner. He'd had to shell out more of his savings to Warson to find out where she'd gone. And now, here he was, asking himself how he'd approach her again without her thinking the worst of him. He hadn't wanted her to see him earlier, it had shocked the shit out of him when she'd looked straight into his eyes and realised who he was. Should he leave her alone for a bit and try again in a couple of weeks? Give her a chance to digest he was here?

But that means she isn't safe. She works with the public. Anything could happen.

No, he'd go back there tonight. Make her understand he only wanted the best for her. They could live somewhere in private, safe. People could visit their house to have a haircut, and he'd be there the whole time to make sure Anna didn't come to any harm. There was her baby to consider now, too. That little boy should be hidden until he grew into a man and could take care of himself.

Children were too vulnerable to be allowed to go outside.

Why doesn't she understand that?

Chapter Nine

In her car, Nessa sat outside Dad's lock-up, situated down a backstreet where other vehicles had been left, belonging to residents farther along around a bend in the road. Binoculars at her eyes, she had a good view through the diamond-wire fencing of the door and window, although a blind covered the glass. An outside light illuminated the surroundings, and a black Transit down the side had a number plate she reckoned was fake—R U R3AD1. *Are you ready.* Stupid, as it was more likely to be noticed if it spelled something out.

He really hasn't *thought this through.*

A quick glance at the time. Ten past midnight.

She shook her head and smiled grimly at his self-assuredness, that he relied on how things *used* to be as opposed to how they worked now. The estate had changed so much since Ron's death, the twins didn't run things the same way, and the players were certainly not who Dad had been used to dealing with. *How* many times had she told him this? Even Ron had given him low-key jobs near the end, preferring to use George and Greg to do the menacing. His way of saying, "Dickie, you're a washed-up has-been."

She jerked more upright at people coming out of the lock-up. Shapes, figures, appearing as dark spectres in the night, smudges of ebony with that light behind them. Several men, most with beer bellies, their clothing black, beanie hats on, although she'd bet they were balaclavas, ready to be pulled down to hide their identities. They milled around, one of them puffing on a cigarette, the smoke rising, curling. Dad locked the door and marched up to the others, saying something, his head bent.

The fact that none of them had clocked her sitting there spoke volumes—they were so up their own arses they didn't think they needed to be careful, they thought their plan was watertight and they were safe to be lax.

But while residents lived around that corner, they weren't loyal to a group of men who used to run with Ron, so any threats sent their way would likely be received with a snort of hilarity, providing guns weren't shoved in their faces. The people around here answered to only two people, the twins, and Dad would realise that if he had to dish out any threats.

She almost wished someone would come along and confront them so she could watch her father being put in his place, being laughed at.

They all climbed into the van, and it reversed onto the street. She held her breath in case it came towards her, the headlights giving away her identity, but it went the other way, towards the houses. She waited a few seconds after they'd gone round the bend, then followed, catching up to them at the junction. She'd tail them to the point she was sure they were going to the salon, then park in the street behind and continue on foot.

Once they began the break-in, she'd tell the twins.

A little shivery thrill went through her at the thought.

Chapter Ten

*R*usty had run around the flat in panic, searching *for a way out. With no windows and the steel exit door, there was no chance of her escaping. She'd screamed, she'd banged on the outer wall in the hope that someone next door, despite the houses being detached, might hear her. She'd drummed her heels on the floor. Smacked her fists against the wall where the painted-over window was behind it. All things, she*

accepted now, were born of desperation and the will to survive. All things she'd expended energy on when she shouldn't have bothered. Her survival instinct had been strong, though. Too strong to ignore.

Her bag, still upstairs in the den, didn't even have a mobile in it. She couldn't afford one and wished to God she'd found a part-time job elsewhere before now so she could have saved for a cheap effort. Come to think of it, she hadn't seen a landline phone upstairs, so even if she did escape this flat and found herself still locked in the house, she couldn't call anyone.

But there were windows up there, she could smash one. Climb out. Run and run and run.

She sat on the sofa, her mind going ten to the dozen, working out how she'd get out of here. They'd come down, wouldn't they? At least to check on her. But Valandra had said no one got out alive, so were they going to starve her to death, just leave her here? Why? What had she done to deserve that? What kind of people were they if incarcerating someone they barely knew was something they did for fun?

She remembered 'our man'. Whoever it was must have been watching her, noting her comings and goings prior to her seeing the job advert in the corner shop window. Did they know enough about her life that her going missing wouldn't particularly be

*noticed by anyone bar her mother? Was he a part of
this, as in, he'd come down here and…and do things to
her? And how could they be sure she'd have even seen
the advert to phone up about the job?*

*It hit her then, how they'd done it, how such an
innocuous conversation, one so easily forgotten until
now, had led to this.*

"Good pay, that," he said, pointing at the advert.

Rusty glanced at the man beside her. She'd already
studied him in the window reflection and hadn't got
any weirdo vibes off him. Jeans, a grubby black T-shirt,
scruffy brown hair and beard. He could be any one of
the residents around here, a bloke nipping to the shop
for his beer and fags.

She smiled and nodded. "Doubt they'd want
anyone like me if they live on Cline. That lot are too
posh."

"Oh, I dunno. Why put the advert in this shop if
they're picky about who looks after their kid? I'd go for
it if I were you. It's not every day you get a chance like
that."

She thought about it. The pay was good—too good.
Or was that the going rate for snobs? People around

here slung you a tenner for watching their children, a token gesture along with a packet of crisps and a can of pop, maybe even providing a hooky DVD to watch.

"I don't know..." She bit her lip. "I'd need to go home and get some money for the phone anyway." She hadn't brought her bag with her.

He dug a hand in his pocket and took two fifty pence coins out. Handed them to her. "I wouldn't hang about. That kind of wage will be snapped up."

Mindful of how every penny counted on this estate, people skint more often than not, she said, "I can't take that."

"I'm not down on my uppers, so go on."

She took the warm coins. "Ta. I only live down the road, so it won't take long for me to get my purse to pay you back once I've—"

"Give over. Just go in there and phone that bleedin' number."

She ignored the butterflies in her stomach and stepped inside. The payphone in the corner seemed to mock her: So you think *you* can get the job, do you? *But the man had given her a pinch of courage, so she asked the woman behind the counter to get the number off the card for her. She made the call, surprised at how easy it was, how nice the child's father had been—Mr*

Flemington. If she wanted the job, it was hers. Could she come to their house on Friday evening?

Back outside, she found the man waiting for her. Not particularly odd—he'd likely want to know how it went, as would many people she knew. It was their way, being invested, if only so they had something to gossip about later. Mind you, no one was interested when it came to making sure she was okay living with an unstable mother, but she supposed everyone had the right to pick and choose who they lent a helping hand to.

"So?" he asked.

"I got the job!"

He smiled. "See? You never know when your fortune's going to change. Good luck now, and maybe I'll see you around." He winked and sauntered off, whistling, seemingly pleased with himself. For doing a good deed?

She didn't know, but God, she had money coming her way.

Maybe life was on the up.

"…and maybe I'll see you around…" A double meaning?

Rusty shuddered. Was he 'our man', as she suspected? It had to be him, didn't it? Leaving it up to chance for her to see that advert—to even need to look for a job in the first place—was too fantastical. They'd engineered this, somehow discovering she needed a job. Who, exactly, had she spoken to about it? When? She couldn't remember. There had been several neighbours she'd asked about babysitting. Had he been listening at some point? He had to have been.

She cast her mind back to the first time she'd come here. Friday evening. Valandra had looked up and down the street—checking to see if anyone was around to note Rusty had gone inside? It was Sunday now, maybe about eight a.m. Mum would have been to the pub last night and probably still slept off the effects of the drink. She wouldn't have a clue Rusty wasn't there. When would she notice? And when she did, what would she do about it?

Desperate not to lose herself in the coming days—she'd acknowledged she'd be here for a while, even if she hadn't quite accepted it; full resignation would inevitably come, though—she went over to the kitchen drawers and opened them one by one to find something she could use to mark the passing days. Something sharp she could carve into the skirting board. Shocked by the contents, and confused, she stared at the knives, the potato masher, the forks and spoons. Everything was there for a usual life, as if they were that confident, they didn't expect her to grab one of those knives and defend herself when they came to visit. If they came.

She opened the top cupboards. Food, more than she'd ever seen at home. Tins, packets of noodles, spaghetti, pasta, jars of sauces. Cereal, long-life milk. A fridge, behind the door of a lower cupboard, contained bacon, butter, ham, cheese, beef, chicken, too many things to wrap her head around.

They planned to keep here here — alive — for at least a fortnight.

What the hell was going on?

She rooted around in the other cupboards. Under the sink, cleaning products, including bleach. That was also a weapon, as was the spray cleaner which would hurt if she pulled the trigger and released fluid into their eyes. She bowed her head, tears stinging — this flat had been stocked up as though she'd be living here like a normal person. Even a washing machine/tumble dryer combo stood behind one of the other unit doors, a cooker beside it. She laughed then, at the irony of that. With only her nightie to her name, it wasn't like she'd be doing the laundry that often, was it.

She checked the rest of the cupboards, bending her head to inspect the waste pipe under the sink. Something had been wedged into the bend. Folded paper? She took it out and, mindful again of cameras, she scooted forward so her body blocked the opening, then opened her find. In the shadowy light, she stared down, leafing through several notebook-sized pages.

Dear Someone Like Me,

If you're reading this, you're either _them_ or someone new. They told me earlier I wouldn't be the last if I didn't give them what they wanted, so I'm writing this in the hope that I can warn you of what's to come, because at least then it won't be such a shock like it was for me. You might find this letter well after you've had your first experience of them using you, but if not, forewarned is forearmed, so my mum says.

I miss her.

I almost saw her today. I was _this close_ to being free. Seems fate or God or destiny, I don't know, have other ideas about my life. I no longer have the taste of freedom on my tongue like I did a few hours ago. I no longer have the energy to fight them. I wish I did. I wish I could escape, but they've proved it'll never happen. They're too clever. Even when they fucked up, they fixed the problem.

I came to babysit, like you might have. I was told to leave Anna alone, to not go upstairs, and now I know why, as do you. They wouldn't want us snooping. But I did—I paid for it later, but I bloody went up there. One of the bedrooms is full of monitors on the wall, a computer on a desk. At the time, I thought it must be something to do with David's work—all the screens were dark, so I had no idea what he might do. Funny how your mind fills in the blanks so it's something plausible. You don't automatically go to the macabre, you justify what you're seeing. I mean, who the hell would believe a posh couple would kidnap people?

Two months after I came down here, they let me know they'd watched me poking around, that they'd filmed me on both nights I babysat.

Have you only babysat twice, too? My theory is they take us on the second night because by then, we trust them. The first night went well, so why wouldn't we? And if we sat for more evenings, there's a risk of us telling people where we've been.

I wish I'd told my mum, but she was away for work at the time I landed the job. There's only me and her, no one else to notice me gone. And that's the beauty of their plan—they chose us, do you understand? We were selected and manipulated to ring that number.

Did they use Anna to get you down here? The ploy that she must have been abducted, then, oh, the relief, she was in the flat, screaming about a spider. A tried-and-tested method, so why would they change it? Were you told she had behavioural issues? That they drugged her so she slept through the night? That a doctor had sanctioned it? He had, but not the usual GP. I'll tell you more about him later.

Anna brought things down for me at first. Bits of shopping. I could have pushed her out of the way and run upstairs, but what was the point? Valandra would be waiting. I'd be strangled until I passed out—David had let me know exactly what would happen in vivid detail. The reason they sent Anna was to isolate me; the first couple of months they just spied on me through their cameras. Yes, they're watching you. Later, Valandra brought the shopping, breezing in as if it's normal to have someone locked downstairs in your house. I'll never forget the way she acted, all nice and kind during those visits, then at night, she flipped a switch and became a monster.

Anna wrote me notes. I think she would have told someone about me if she could, but she doesn't go to school, so who could she tell? I worry about her, hidden in this house. Valandra educates her, but one day that child is going to wonder why she can't go out like other kids. She's going to grow into an adult who'll have questions and needs. Are they going to let her go to college, knowing what she knows, how she can get them right in the shit?

David and Valandra live a strange and frightening life. She _is_ a photographer, she's not lying there. She _does_ make a lot of money. David does, too, but I have no idea what his profession is, he's never said.

There was someone else before me, and she died. Her name was Lacey-Louise Barker, David told me — please remember that, because if you get out, her family need to know what happened. David and Valandra found her in the shower, the water still spraying on her, wrists slashed.

I often wonder how I'll go. Whether I'll kill myself or if they'll do it for me.

Anna will be the only friend you have from now on, if she's even allowed to come down and see you after what she did for me. Be kind to her — she's as much a prisoner as you are, obeying them because that's all she's ever known. She's David's child but not Valandra's — Lacey is her mother. Valandra can't have babies. Before Lacey died, she gave birth to Anna on the floor. The doctor had come. He'd taken Valandra to register the birth — he'd forged all the prenatal visits so it looked like she was the mother. They are evil, evil *people, with one goal in mind: to have children then dispose of the mother once the breastfeeding stage is over.*

Will I have a child? Will Valandra wear her fake pregnancy belly again to fool everyone that she's the mother? She finds that funny, you know, tricking everyone. Getting all the attention that comes with having a baby. Telling me all about how they've hoodwinked the world. You'll come to find she loves talking about herself. She's self-absorbed and dangerous, so don't let her little chats fool you, especially the ones about her childhood.

I lied. They don't only have one goal in mind. Before the pregnancy, they'll use you, both of them, in sick, twisted sex games. They'll film you tied up. Valandra will take photos. Did you go in the den? I bet you stayed there on your second night, didn't you. Those pictures on the wall — they're Lacey. Her eye, her hand, her backside, and on the landing down here, her feet with the dark polish. If you disobeyed them and went upstairs, you'll have seen more. A mouth, a hand covering a breast, the length of her back, her shoulder blades sticking out where she must have tried to starve herself to death.

Maybe my pictures have been added to the walls by the time you're reading this. Maybe my hair has been woven into the potpourri like hers. Maybe my initials are carved beneath one of those wooden faces on the mantelpiece. Did you spot that?

She went through hell, and so have I.

I don't know what else to say other than be prepared for the worst life can throw at you. Don't take the bait if Anna tries to help you escape—they'll likely use her now to trick you, to see if you've still got it in you to run. But the most upsetting thing of all for me is 'our man'. He will come. He will watch while they treat you like a sex slave. He will laugh and hurt you for fun. He's David's brother, and he's as fucked-up as they are.

He's the doctor.

My real name is Shania Peterson. I lived at 78 Windermere Gardens. I am eighteen.

I don't think I'll ever get to be any older.

I'll pray for you.

Good luck, and I hope you manage to escape.

Shania

xxx

A big wave of fear swept over Rusty, combined with sadness and revulsion. So much information to take in. A story of horror, sadness, and such vileness she couldn't comprehend it. What was it David had said?

Using your brain to get what you want, mapping it all out. They must have planned this to the nth degree, every avenue inspected for flaws.

Had Shania almost got away? It sounded as if she had. Anna had been involved—had they sent her down here to set her free, then they'd hunted her down for sport? Shania's warning rang through her mind—don't take the bait…

Who the hell had come up with this scheme? Which one of them had spoken the first dreadful words: We should kidnap people to have our children. *What kind of depraved bastards were they to live such a hideous dual life? She'd never have believed people were capable of this if she hadn't been studying criminology, and on some level she'd blocked it out, the true disgust of this kind of situation. It happened, she knew that, but in suburbia, one of the players a well-known photographer, the second a God-knew-what, and the third…the doctor, the man who'd encouraged her to phone the number.*

Lacey had killed herself. What had they done with the body? They must have dumped it. Had they planned for that eventuality, too, right down to where her grave would be? She thought of the Porsche's clean tyres. Had they taken Shania off and buried her, then changed the tyres so no evidence was on them?

That level of scheming scared the shit out of her, and it must have been recent, because the tyres had still been black at the edges. Shania couldn't have got pregnant—there was only Anna here. And that poor child. How could they trust her not to say anything when they involved her in this mess? She'd passed notes to Shania—she must be good at English for an eight-year-old. Did she write notes because the flat was riddled with cameras and they'd hear her talking? How had she passed them over without being caught on tape?

Rusty folded the note and put it back in the U-bend. If she was being watched right now, what did they think she'd been doing while she'd read the letter? Maybe having a moment to assimilate her situation?

Paranoia took hold. What if there was a camera under the sink? What if Shania didn't exist and David or Valandra had written the letter? What if this was all part of their fucked-up game?

She stood, her legs sore from kneeling, and continued her exploration of the flat in case they were watching. On the outside, she'd appear as they'd expect, someone getting to know their surroundings, but inside her head, she sifted through the information and tried to work out what to do about it. Use Anna to pass a note to someone living in the street? Or was the child watched like a hawk and wouldn't be able to leave the house? Anna had told Rusty to run, so she knew what went on here was bad. Despite being brought up by insane parents who could have warped her mind to their way of thinking, the child knew right from wrong.

There was hope for her, then.

In the bedroom, she opened the built-in wardrobe. A rail of clothes, and below, a chest of drawers. She pulled the top one open — new packets of knickers. Bras, socks, everything a person could need. A shiver crawled up her spine — this was so creepy, the way they'd designed this so it looked as if Rusty was down here of her own accord. She could live like everyone else, with the knives to cut sandwiches, the bleach to squirt down the toilet.

What the hell would they do in order for her not to attack them? Because that filled her mind now, drawing blood, watching them bleed out to ensure they were dead, then taking Anna to safety. What would they say to make her comply to their wishes so she didn't use those knives? Threaten to hurt Mum? Hurt Rusty? Pull a gun on her?

She moved around casually, glancing surreptitiously to find cameras. If there were any, they'd been hidden well, but she sensed those lenses trained on her, as if they followed her from room to room. As if David, Valandra, and 'our man' knew exactly what she was doing.

Chapter Eleven

Anna woke to the God-awful sound of banging. The walls buzzed with it, and she sat up, her chest heavy with fear. A quick glance at Harper's cot showed him out for the count, but if the racket kept on, he'd wake soon. What was it? Roadworks? Were they *allowed* to make that much noise at night?

Shaking, she got up and went to the window. Stared down into the street in front of the salon. A quick glance left and right showed nothing untoward. The alley over the road stood in darkness, a black slice between the backs of the buildings. Will's car sat at the kerb reassuringly, and she was surprised no one had come to relieve him yet. He caught sight of her and waved.

She collected her phone from the nightstand and messaged him.

ANNA: CAN YOU HEAR THAT NOISE?

WILL: I CAN NOW. I HAD MY EARBUDS IN. BRING HARPER DOWN TO THE CAR, QUICKLY. I'LL TEXT GG.

Could he see something she couldn't? She panicked at a loud rumble, and this time, it was clear either her salon or another shop along the row was being broken into. She put on her dressing gown and slippers, dropped her phone and the hidey-hole remote control in her pocket, and lifted Harper, draping a blanket over him. He slept on, and she shuddered—*she'd* slept like the dead as a child, too, except *he* hadn't been drugged.

She crept down the stairs to the short, narrow hallway and took her handbag off the wall hook. She bypassed the locked steel door that led to the salon. She had no pressing need to investigate whether the rear of the shop was the target—and if it was, someone must have found out about the secret panel. It reminded her to use the remote. She unlocked her private front door and stepped into the street, Will there to take Harper from her. She closed the door and stood at one of the large windows, pointed the remote at it, and clicked the reinforcement button. As well as a steel panel, George's workmen had returned to add iron bars behind the office wall, so if they got through that far, they'd be further hampered by having to cut through them, giving George and Greg more time to get here, the salon alarm alerting them there was a problem. She always ensured those bars were activated when she locked up, but she'd pressed that button again to be sure.

The alarm. It wasn't blaring. Maybe it wasn't this shop being raided? But which shop was it, and why wasn't *that* alarm going off?

Fear slicing through her, she rushed across the street and got in the back of Will's car, picking up a stirring Harper and securing them with the seat belt. If they got caught and he wasn't in a baby seat, there'd be trouble, but that was the least of her worries now.

"They must be round the back," Will said. "God help them when the twins get here."

She recalled her earlier thought, that Greg might be dead, but if Will had mentioned them both, she'd probably got it wrong. So where *was* Greg the past couple of weeks? Or was Will in on the subterfuge, mentioning them as a duo so she didn't think twice about it? If George hadn't told her Greg had been shot, she wouldn't be questioning it.

Will drove off, checking the rearview, his eyes narrowed. His features appeared tense, as if he witnessed something, and she didn't dare turn around to see. He shook his head, smiled, and concentrated on the road.

"Where are we going?" she asked.

"I've been instructed to get you out of the vicinity. We're going to a safe house."

"But I haven't got enough nappies or anything. I've got one in my handbag, but that's not enough."

"George said to stop at the twenty-four-hour Tesco on the way. He'll buy whatever you need. I've been given a Monzo card—he's put some money on it for emergencies and my expenses, food and whatnot. I got an Uber Eats to deliver to my car earlier."

She hadn't spotted that, too busy getting Harper his dinner then giving him a bath, although she *had* been peering out every now and then to ensure Will was still there. While she trusted George to do as he'd promised, she didn't know him that well, and her past meant she didn't truly trust *anyone*.

The scenery whizzed by, the orange light from streetlamps flashing stripes on Harper's head periodically. The houses stood in darkness, everyone in bed, although some people walked up roads, maybe coming back from a night out. She recalled her time in Manchester as an adult, how she'd thought nothing of leaving pubs and clubs by herself, not caring one way or the other if she was beaten up or abducted. Life had held no meaning back then, she hadn't cared about herself at all, because her experiences had proved that no one else had cared for her either, so why should she? Her reason for living hadn't arrived until she'd found out she was pregnant. Only then had she wanted to do better, to bring Harper up surrounded by love, not the invisible iron bars she'd received.

What if it *was* the salon being raided? How cruel fate was; she'd only just opened it, and now it might have to be closed if they trashed the place. The robbers might be the type to not only take what was behind the wall panel but go into the salon itself and mindlessly wreck it.

"I *knew* something like this would happen," she blurted, anger and sadness looping together. "I said to myself that those workmen might not be trustworthy. One of them was weird, staring at me funny. I told George, but he said he's used them for years and they're one of the crews."

"Yeah, they have different teams for things. Like building, cleaning up the warehouse, stuff like that."

"The warehouse?"

He looked at her in the rearview. "Ah, you don't know about that, then."

"Um, no. Do I want to?"

"It'll be where your man gets taken when they catch up with him. I'll leave it to the twins to tell you. Not my place to gossip."

Will drove on, and Anna got thumped with the knowledge she had a lot to learn about The Brothers.

Chapter Twelve

Ichabod waited in the darkness, annoyed at the fact Will had clocked him as he'd driven away. He told himself to be more careful in future. The last thing he needed was his target to spot where he was. The man could bolt down the other end of the alley and lose himself in the maze of streets. Ichabod sighed and, phone in the shade of his jacket front to stop too much light being revealed, he sent a message.

ICHABOD: HE'S COME TO THE SALON ON FOOT. HIDING DOWN AN ALLEY OPPOSITE. ANNA'S JUST GONE WITH WILL.

GG: WE'LL GET HOLD OF JANINE—SHE CAN HAVE A WORD WITH HIM AS WE'RE A BIT TIED UP. WE'LL ARRANGE A PLACE FOR YOU TO MEET. STAND BY FOR MORE INSTRUCTIONS.

Chapter Thirteen

Nessa had seen enough. Dad and his gang had failed to break the door down with the ram and now used some kind of battery-operated saw to cut into the wood around the handle. In the alley behind the shops' yards, she walked quietly, although the noise from the saw was enough to drown out her footsteps. She reached the end and turned right into the Spar car park, running past the Transit. She rushed to the next road along and got in her car.

Dad was an utter twat. She experienced no guilt at what she was about to do. When she considered how he'd treated her, casting her aside because she wasn't a boy, he deserved everything he got. She'd act like a son now, a *man*, and use her bollocks to get him caught. He'd never think she'd have it in her, what with her being a mere girl.

NESSA: MY DAD'S BEEN ACTING SUSS LATELY, SO I FOLLOWED HIM TONIGHT. HE'S BREAKING INTO YOUR FUCKING HAIRDRESSER'S!

GG: WE KNOW. EN ROUTE. HOW MANY PRESENT?

NESSA: SIX. ONE OF THEM IS JORDY ROBINSON, DON'T KNOW WHO THE REST ARE.

GG: GET YOURSELF HOME. YOU DON'T WANT TO SEE YOUR OLD MAN GUNNED DOWN.

NESSA: MAKE SURE THE BULLETS HIT THE MARK.

GG: FUCK ME, HAVE YOU GOT A BEEF WITH HIM?

NESSA: THE WHOLE FUCKING COW.

GG: GEORGE TOLD ME TO SAY THANKS FOR THE INFO.

NESSA: MAYBE I'LL BE ALLOWED TO BE NICE TO HIM NOW.

GG: EH?

NESSA: NOTHING.

She dropped her phone into the cupholder and drove towards home. How odd that she didn't care that her father would be killed tonight. How un-daughter-like to smile at the thought of it, to wish she could be there to see the light of fear in his eyes when he realised what was happening. If he'd been kinder to her, maybe she'd have let him live, but he'd pissed her off one time too many earlier, his final, spiteful comments breaking the camel's back.

"Fuck you, old man. Fuck. You."

She laughed until she cried.

Chapter Fourteen

Dickie, frustrated as fuck, drew the front of his balaclava up so he could get some air to his clammy face. He was sweating like a pig, his armpits oily with it. He'd already checked for cameras out here and found none, so he wasn't bothered about his face being seen, although Nessa would point out that he should be, that the twins weren't stupid, they'd have tiny cameras embedded in the bricks, not easily seen. She'd got right on his nerves earlier tonight, pointing out pitfalls, as if he wasn't clever enough to work these things out for himself. Who the hell did she think she was?

He cursed the fact she'd been right. Did she have inside information? She'd warned him this might happen, and he hadn't listened. The battering ram had been next to useless, and the saw wasn't much cop either. Sparks flew as the blade chomped into something beneath the wood—reinforced steel most likely. His man who'd come to watch the hairdresser's being renovated hadn't passed on about the metal. The little prick would pay for that. Or was he in the twins' employ, told to lie and say the place wasn't Fort Knox like Nessa had said?

Should I be wary of her?

Nah, she wouldn't dare cross him. She'd been scared of him all her life, as had her mother, the insipid woman he loved to bully because she was so damn submissive. He'd thought she was a fiery one when he'd first met her, she'd had a gob on her, and him barking at her hadn't been to dull that spirit but enhance it. Beverly hadn't got the memo, she'd cowered instead of fighting back. No wonder he'd gone off with another woman.

"Put some welly into it," he snapped. "How thick *is* that steel?"

"I can't get through," Big John said.

"'Ere, let me have a go." Little John snatched at the saw.

"Oi," Big John barked.

"Shut up," Dickie hissed. "People live in the flats above the shops."

When the alarm had been sorted without a hitch, he'd thought this would be plain sailing, fate on his side like it had been when he'd worked for Ron, everything clicking into place. A fortune in their hands. That fortune slipped away the longer he stood and stared at those mocking sparks. Seeing as they hadn't even breached the back door yet, his anger levels rose. All that racket they were making would alert someone, and he didn't fancy a shootout if nosy beaks came poking around. Nicking was one thing, but he didn't want anyone using a gun unless it was absolutely necessary. He trusted the fella he'd bought them from—to a degree—but there hadn't been any assurance that they hadn't been used in other crimes. If they got caught after killing people, the other offences would be pinned on them.

Shit, this crap was harder than he remembered.

The sensible side of him said to go home, put it down to a lost cause, but the greedy side, the one who wanted all that lovely money from the sale of guns and drugs, told him to let his mates carry on for a bit longer.

But if they got caught…

"I'm calling it off." He put a hand on Little John's arm.

"I did wonder when you'd pipe up with the right decision," Jordy sniped from beside him. "Fuck my old boots, anyone can see we're not getting inside there. You should have listened to Nessa."

Dickie bristled. "I didn't see you stepping in to back her up."

"Yeah, well, you'd have shot *me* down an' all. Fuck this, I'm out of here." Jordy tromped down the yard, opening the gate and walking into the alley.

Dickie sighed. His temper would get the better of him if he had to see Jordy's smug grin anytime soon, so instead of following him to give him a punch, he helped pack the saw up to give him some breathing space. With one last, forlorn look at the door that only had damage to the wooden façade and a scratch to the steel, he led his mates away from the goldmine and down the alley. Halfway along, he had the urge to nip down the side alley to the left, go round the front and try smashing the windows, but he pushed it back. A mug's game—and Nessa would probably be right there, too. Reinforced glass.

A BMW crept past the street opening, and Dickie about shit his kecks.

"Shit, the twins are here. Get moving."

Someone bumped into him from behind, and Dickie's dentures shot out. They clattered on the ground, and he peered into the blackness to find them.

"Me teef," he said. "I've gone and losh me fuggin' teef."

"Fuck them," Big John barked. "We need to go."

They carried on down the alley behind the shops, Dickie out of breath, his lips flapping by the time they reached the end. He pulled his balaclava back down—there'd be CCTV cameras here. They darted into the empty Spar car park and tumbled into the van, Jordy already in the back. The driver gunned the engine and sped off, Dickie's heart going mental. He panted, his face hot and sweaty again, and glanced over at Jordy who held his phone beneath his chin, lighting his face up like some macabre Halloween mask.

"You're such a childish wanker," Dickie grumbled. "Pack it in."

"Why, have a heart attack, did you?"

"We're not nineteen anymore, so don't go playing games." Dickie snatched the balaclava off, glad of the cool air swarming around his head. "The fucking twins showed up, didn't they. Us sorting that alarm must have tripped something."

"We knew we'd have twenty minutes max before either they or the police came along. You act like you're surprised." Jordy shone his phone torch at Dickie. "I thought you sounded funny. Where's your teeth?"

"They fell out. Some prick" —he glared around at the others—"barged into me."

Jordy laughed, his head thudding against the side of the van. "Oh, fuck me, that's classic, that is. You'd better hope the twins don't find them. They're going to know they're yours. I did say not

138

to get a gold tooth in the front because it singles you out, but you wouldn't have any of it."

"Fuck off, you sound like Nessa." Dickie folded his arms. "And get that fucking torch off me."

No one spoke for the rest of the way to the lock-up. Dickie, livid they wouldn't be lugging bags of coke, weed, and guns in there, got out and opened the lock-up door, stomping inside. Everyone else joined him, and they stripped out of their black clothes and put their suits back on.

"What a fucking shit shower," Dickie said, calculating how much cash he could generate from the goods inside the cardboard boxes all around the edge, containing bent gear. He'd promised his mistress a trip to Marbella after this, and he wasn't going to give that up.

"Yeah, well…" Jordy left the rest of his words in his mouth.

Fucking good job, else Dickie would've decked him if he'd carried on.

"Keep your thoughts to yourself." Dickie punched his palm.

Jordy laughed. "You forget, I'm not scared of you."

Dickie hated not being feared as much as he used to be. God, he missed those heady days with Ron, fucking about like no one's business, shitting the life out of people. Until those bastard twins had come along and nabbed all the good jobs. And they'd ruined *this* job, too.

Someone needed to take them out.

He smiled. Maybe that was a scheme for another day.

Chapter Fifteen

*A*nna slept soundly, and Valandra was downstairs cooking dinner. In the upstairs observation room, David zoomed in on Rusty. She lay in bed, staring at the ceiling, directly into the camera lens in the chandelier. As if she stared straight at him. A shiver of delight wound through him—he'd get to see her staring at him for real soon, right into his eyes, the terror in hers palpable. He hadn't been down there since he'd locked the door on Sunday morning. Monday had rolled round, and he'd gone to work as usual in his Porsche, swearing he could smell Shania's dead-body scent wafting from the boot, even though he'd valeted the life out of it.

Rusty had settled in faster than the other two. It seemed she'd become resigned to her fate already, although what that fate was, she had no idea. He couldn't wait for her to twig that she wasn't being held down there as a kidnap victim.

The dawning of the truth always hit hard. He'd seen it so much at work, where the moment reality hit them, they crumpled. So often, they collapsed, their legs unable to hold them up. They shook, cried, shouted, couldn't breathe, all manner of things really. A good study, those people, because they'd given him an insight into how their captives might react, the levels of emotion to expect, and how they should deal with it.

Lacey had been meek and mild, even when presented with her future. She hadn't had an ounce of fight in her. They'd chosen her because of her demeanour — no sense in entering their first foray with a feisty bitch, too complicated, so a quiet one had been the order of the day to ease them in. The sex games had been ruined because of it, though. She didn't push them away, just cried and let them get on with it, and while that wasn't *exactly thrilling, he and Valandra had been excited all the same. It had been new, using another woman against her will, but the novelty had worn off, and they'd craved someone who hated them, who fought them all the way.*

She'd given them Anna, which he'd forever be grateful for. Valandra couldn't have children and, desperate as she'd been to become a mother, his brother, Sidney, had suggested they get a surrogate. In his profession, he had the means to put them in touch with various people in the know, but the cost was exorbitant. They could afford it, especially as Valandra's photography had taken off to such a staggering degree, but why spend so much when you could get it for free? In a private conversation, Valandra excluded, Sidney had mentioned a man and wife who'd allowed the surrogate to come and live with them throughout the pregnancy.

"What if you did the same, put her in Mum's flat?"

The idea had been born, and together, they'd plotted, just like they had when their mother had lived down there. That bitch had paid for the upbringing she'd given them, Sidney well aware of how to kill her without anyone knowing—a slow, painful death, the poison undetected in blood tests. So handy, having a GP for a sibling.

David chuckled. The pair of them were ruthless bastards, even they acknowledged that, and it had been a revelation when they'd met Valandra, someone as unhinged as them. At the time, he'd fancifully wondered whether fate was a real thing and had sent her their way, birds of a feather flocking together, but it had been a coincidence that she'd also been brought up in a world where getting what she wanted, whichever way she could, was her MO. She felt owed, like he and Sidney had, and over the years they'd become a trio of fiends, sharing their sexual encounters, Sidney never touching Valandra but watching, always watching from the corner, his dick in hand.

Going to swinger parties had grown old. Not to mention too much risk, given Valandra's sudden local fame, David's higher position at work, and also Sidney's standing in the community. Taking a young woman off the street and using her to their hearts' content had been a logical step, until she became pregnant, then they nurtured so the foetus had the best chance of survival.

Some would say they were depraved, and those people would be correct. The normal side of David knew right from wrong. The abnormal side didn't care once he was in the throes of a plan. As a police superintendent, he knew only too well what others would label them—perverts, self-centred deviants, people who should be locked up, the key thrown down a deep, dark well. But he couldn't help himself, none of them could. Once they'd dipped a toe into the forbidden waters, there had been no going back. Their former lives had appeared mundane.

They'd lied to Rusty, telling her their man had looked into her, although Sidney had followed her around in disguise. It had been David checking the police database initially. Sidney had convinced her at the corner shop to phone that babysitting number. The rough-and-ready accent he'd spoken with when giving her the coins had been enough to convince her he was someone like her, your average resident.

How easy it had been.

He stared at the monitor. A tear slipped from her eye, down her temple to sink into the pillow. What was she thinking? About her slovenly mother who, in a couple of hours, would take a man home, too in her cups to see him clearly, to remember him. After Sidney had finished with her, she'd be fit for no one in the bedroom for a while, a wedge of money left on her bedside table, him telling her she should drink herself to death and be done with it. With the amount of cash they'd agreed she could have, she'd manage to stumble to the off-licence, as alcoholics always could despite the state of them, and at least drink herself into oblivion for a few days. Enough time for Rusty being missing to be forgotten. Until she realised, and they had that covered. Sidney would pack some of Rusty's clothes and leave a note, one Valandra had forced her to write yesterday. She was leaving for university early.

No one would report Rusty missing.

Perfect.

Valandra loved the anticipation of this bit, where she had minimal contact with the future mother and left her to stew. Yesterday, she'd broken the two-month 'ignore the captive' rule, going in to encourage her to write a note. It had spoiled the joy somewhat. David had insisted, though—Rusty's mother, Katherine, may well be an alcoholic mess, but she relied on her daughter, and Rusty going missing would be seen as odd if it went on for much longer. Although they'd abducted her at the weekend, the most likely time Katherine would be drunk out of her mind, too sozzled to even notice her daughter's absence, she would notice it by midweek. She'd wonder where her meals had gone, where her clean clothes were. That awful woman didn't know what a diamond of a daughter she had. She ought to be more grateful.

Tonight, Sidney was doing the honours—he had such a wicked slant to his personality, and what he planned to do to the woman in bed almost had Valandra wishing she was there to see it first-hand. He'd hurt her—a lot—and Katherine might think twice about taking a stranger home in the future.

She imagined him with his fake beard, the wig covering his usually close-shaven head, contacts in instead of his trademark glasses, the dreadful clothes he'd undoubtedly put on as opposed to his snappy workday suits. She loved him—not like she loved David, who she was in love with—but she had a deep affection for Sidney, a man she found incredibly attractive. She loved how he watched her having sex with his brother, how the three of them were so cohesive and on the same page.

She'd got lucky the day she'd met those two in that wine bar. They'd been on the prowl, that much had been obvious, and after a few drinks, Valandra more than tipsy, David had whispered what they wanted. A threesome, but only David would touch her. That night had birthed their relationship, one that had grown from strength to strength over the years. It electrified her to live two lives—one they presented to the outside world, another they kept hidden.

She finished loading the dishwasher and wandered to the bottom of the stairs. One hand on the newel post, she thought of Rusty down there, alone, frightened. By the time Valandra and David visited her again, she would be so desperate for human interaction that she'd be pliable enough to do get her to do whatever they wanted, although David would hope she put up a fight. He'd scare her silly with his fake gun to ensure she behaved.

She climbed the stairs, peeking in on Anna, who slept soundly. Sidney's prescriptions had been a lifesaver. No one wanted a child walking in on them having sex, especially not when the uncle sat there in the corner.

She walked to the observation room doorway and leaned on the jamb. David sat and watched Rusty, his elbows on the desk, hands clasped into a double fist beneath his chin. The light from the screen pasted his features, showing how relaxed they were, how content he was.

"I know you're there," he said.

"Dinner's ready."

He nodded. Shut the feed down. All the monitors winked out.

"I'm worried she'll be like Lacey," he said and stood to stretch the knots out of his back, ones he complained about if he sat up here for too long. "She's apathetic too soon."

"The fire will come back, you'll see. Look how crazy she went when we first left her there. She wanted to tear down the walls."

"It should have lasted longer than that. Her personality is feistier than Shania's, and you remember how many days—days, my darling—she railed for. Why has Rusty seemed to accept what's going on? You know how I like to understand the intricacies of the mind, so it's a question that's been bothering me."

Valandra tittered. "Come now, she studies criminology. She knows how to behave to get us to think she's compliant. She'll suspect that's what we want—no way would she imagine we actually enjoy the fight. She'll wait, bide her time, play the good little victim, then pick her moment to escape. What she doesn't know is we want her to take a knife from that drawer and try to stab us with it."

"That sounds so deranged when you put it like that."

"Good job you know exactly what I mean then, isn't it."

She led the way downstairs, thinking of all the lovely pictures she'd take of Rusty, ones where she couldn't be identified. She'd sell them, like all the others, the purchasers having no idea that the art they'd bought was of people incarcerated on the bottom floor of their house. Such depravity would never be suspected.

At the dining table, she took the lids off the dishes and served herself—David didn't want her to be the little wife at home who tended to his every whim, and if he had, he'd have had a long wait. She tended to no one unless she wanted to—those days were over.

She shoved away thoughts of her childhood and ate some cauliflower, then cut into her bloody steak. David dished up his food and poured red wine. She'd cook Sidney his steak when he arrived later—he'd be hungry after tonight's exertions.

"Do you think Anna will ever be able to go to school?" she asked.

Much as she was sick and twisted, she hated the idea of their child being denied a normal life. They did take her out, to the zoo, theme parks, and she had the odd McDonald's, but Anna's life was far from the usual — and it wasn't because they were afraid she'd spill the beans, because as far as Anna was concerned, there were no beans to spill. David had craved having a child so much he'd wanted to wrap her up in cotton wool, keep her away from people who could harm her. Like Valandra had been harmed. Valandra had been inclined to agree, but Anna was missing out on so many life experiences.

She paused with her fork midair. "I know you don't want to manipulate her to the point she becomes aware that what we do is wrong and she has to cover it up, but there will come a time when she naturally wonders why she isn't like other children. She watches television, she knows kids go to school and she doesn't. What will you tell her when she asks why she can't go?"

"Say it isn't safe? You could use the shootings in America as a lesson. Lay down the ground rules so she's too afraid to want to go to school."

"Cruel, don't you think?"

He laughed. "We're cruel people, or has that slipped your mind? I will do whatever it takes to keep her safe and protected. I couldn't bear to lose her. She could be taken away from us by a pervert…"

"Like we've taken other mothers' children?" She raised an eyebrow.

"That's different, they're adults."

"It isn't different at all. We are exactly the people you fear. At the moment, Anna doesn't realise what she's doing for us is aiding and abetting. A child will do as they're told, without question for the most part, so us telling her to go downstairs and pretend there's a spider to scare the babysitter... Not exactly anything to cause her alarm, is it. She believes the women are renting from us, and when we send her down there with little messages, she has no clue what they actually mean. 'Change the bedsheets' is just an instruction she's been told to give them, but our mothers-to-be know it's the signal for us going down there to fuck them senseless."

They'd been so careful to bring Anna up oblivious, but what if Rusty didn't get pregnant and they had to dispose of her and find another woman? These things took time and a lot of planning. Time that meant Anna would be much older when the next babysitter came and might notice more things being off. She was eight now, and Valandra wanted a new baby so there wasn't a big age gap. They'd have had one if Shania had produced what they wanted, but she hadn't. Wasting months, hoping David's seed took root, had been a fraught time.

Valandra tried again. "As Anna's so shielded from all this, I really don't see why she can't live a more normal life. Yes, I know your sister was abducted and murdered when she was five, but what are the chances of it happening to Anna, too?"

"I don't want to take the risk." He smiled at her. Chilling. "Darling, you agreed to the rules before we had her. You said you'd school her from home."

"I can't school her at a higher level when the time comes. She's so clever, so gifted, and she's not going to want to miss out on college or university. We're not good parents if we deny her that right. And she'll become an adult, able to make her own decisions. What will you do, lock her in the flat so she can't ever leave?"

"I've thought about it."

Valandra gaped at him. "That's a step too far. You know how I felt while growing up. I lived on that bloody farm in the middle of nowhere, isolated, lonely, and desperate for friends. How can I inflict the same life on Anna, knowing what it was like?"

"She won't be used to milk the cows and do manual labour. She'll be treated like a princess." He paused to cock his head at her. "Are cracks showing, darling? Do I need to be worried about your feelings?"

She shook her head; she'd gone too far and would leave this subject alone for now. This side of him had become more apparent lately, and it had shown her he might not be all he seemed. "No, of course not. After all, she isn't my child, so what I say doesn't matter."

It had always irked her that she hadn't carried Anna, hadn't pushed her out of her body—she was only saying what David might come out with next, a reminder that she didn't have a legal say in how Anna was brought up, despite Valandra's name being on the birth certificate.

Sometimes, as much as she felt she'd found her true soul mates in David and Sidney, she wished she hadn't met them. Hadn't known what it was like to fall so desperately in love that she'd go to the levels she had. It was one thing for her to throw herself into this insane life, to want the thrills and excitement, but another when a child was involved.

She could only pray Anna would grow up well-adjusted and wouldn't hate them for keeping her locked away. Like Valandra had hated her parents.

So much so, she'd set the farmhouse alight with them in it and walked away.

Chapter Sixteen

By the time George and Greg made it to the back of the salon, Dickie and his lot had gone. George seethed. If it hadn't been for a snarl-up because of an accident on the way here and them having to take a detour, they'd have caught them red-handed. They'd left home as soon as Will's message had come through, mentioning loud bangs. Nessa's had arrived a few minutes later.

Why hadn't she messaged at the same time as Will? George imagined she may have been struck by indecision—grassing your old man up was considered heartless by some, but those people casting aspersions had the luxury of having a nice dad, so they couldn't *imagine* grassing on him. Or had she needed to get away before she could alert them? The light of her phone screen would have given her away.

With the group of men not here, had Nessa got an attack of the guilts and warned Dickie to get away? Nah, it had come across loud and clear that she wanted him dead, so that couldn't be it. Annoyed at having to always second-guess everything, George paced the yard. He got on the phone to one of the crew members who'd come and put a new façade on the door tomorrow. Anna was at the safe house with Will and Harper, so that was one less thing to worry about, and she'd stay there until the morning.

Conversation finished, he said to Greg, "We'll station Will in the salon all day tomorrow if we haven't got hold of Dickie and his geriatric mob by then—the sofa's due to arrive at nine. Anna's not going to want to stay closed until they're caught, not when she's only just opened."

Greg nodded. "Right. Let's check down the alley, see where they could have parked that van. Will didn't report any Transits coming down the street, nor a group of blokes going down the alley between the shops, so it wouldn't have been there."

"I had horrible thoughts about Nessa."

"Like what?"

"Her message coming in much later than Will's. My mind went to the dark side."

"Good, it means you're watching your back more. But she informed on her own father, so that should tell you something. She might have driven off somewhere safe before she picked up the blower."

George directed his phone torch beam ahead and led the way out of the yard. He paused at the gate. "They snipped our fucking padlock." Annoyed by that and putting it on his mental list to replace the whole gate in the morning to a better one, he went right, scarfing the beam back and forth on the tarmac path. Seeing nothing, he retraced his steps, Greg in front of him now. "Get behind me."

Greg tutted, putting his own torch on and aiming the light at George's face. "For Christ's *sake*, bruv, I put a *vest* on."

George battled with his need to protect. "Fine." But it wasn't.

They walked past the salon and a couple of other shops, then Greg stopped.

"The twat's left his teeth."

George stepped to his brother's side and stared down. The gold incisor winked in the torchlight. "*I'm* not picking them up. He can stay gummy for all I care." He kicked them out of the way.

They strode on, discovering the empty Spar car park.

"They'll have come here," George said.

"Hmm. We'll send someone round first thing to get that CCTV wiped. We don't want the pigs knowing where they were and following the trail."

George frowned. "Why would the pigs even come?"

"One of the residents in the flats above the shops is bound to have phoned them by now. I doubt they'll arrive for a while as the police are thin on the ground."

George scratched his head. "They might nose about and see the door at the back of the salon."

"So?"

"They could drop by tomorrow and ask Anna why anyone would want to rob a hairdresser's. Be suspicious that there's more on the premises when they discover we're the ones who own it. I mean, what would thieves be after, a few pairs of fucking scissors?"

"There's the dryers, the chairs, all the dyes. Someone who wants to open up their own business but doesn't want to fork out for the stuff. Don't sweat it."

"Yeah, well, I do. That woman's been through enough, she doesn't need more on her plate to get antsy about."

"Maybe we should open up another salon and stick her in there, then, if you're worried. Why take her on if she's got issues?"

"I didn't fucking *know* she had issues at the time, did I. God. I thought I'd missed you picking at me but…"

Greg elbowed him. "Shut your face, I'm winding you up."

George released a breath. "What a knob."

Back out the front, he swiped his gaze across the road at the alley. The mouth of it, a dark pit, hid Bastard in its shadows. What was the man thinking? Was he going to wait until they'd gone, then go home? With Anna out of the picture, there was no point in him being here. George looked elsewhere in search of Ichabod, but the man was a chameleon and blended in with wherever he'd positioned himself.

Satisfied the Irishman had everything in hand, he pondered how Dickie's lot had managed to tamper with the alarm. There were no visible wires, nor was there an alarm box. Did they have some kind of jamming device? If so, who'd given it to them? Whoever it was would know it was for something dodgy, and if they lived on Cardigan and George found out who it was, he'd be gunning for them. Aiding and abetting deserved a kneecapping at the very least.

His suspicion gene woke up. Who'd told them what was stored in the salon? Had one of the crew opened their mouths after years of keeping it closed? Had the alarm company employee been compromised? He didn't for one second think it had been Anna, but he'd keep the possibility in mind because he'd been bitten in the past.

"Reckon Dickie still lives in the same place?" Greg asked as they got in the car.

"Dunno, but I know where the lock-up is. What's the betting they're there? If they're not, we'll burn the place to the ground, then go round his gaff. If he's moved, we'll find out where he's gone from Nessa." George clipped his seat belt in and drove away.

"There's got to be some bad blood between them if she grassed him up." Greg strapped in. "I mean, fuck me sideways..."

"Dickie's always been a dick—did you like what I did there? Imagine living with him. That poor Beverly. D'you remember that time she came to Ron's Portakabin asking where her old man was because he hadn't been home for days?"

"Yeah, and Ron was his usual arsehole self and told her Dickie was shagging that Marlborough woman, the posh one we used to piss off by egging her house."

George laughed. He'd forgotten about that. "Bloody hell, what a memory. Wonder why Beverly puts up with him."

"She might be like Mum. *She* put up with more than anyone should. Dickie's likely a controlling bastard."

"Not for much longer." George pulled up behind a small white van and stared across at the lock-up. He was going to kill those fuckers and enjoy doing it. "You'd think they'd be a bit more savvy by not having that outside light on."

"They won't think anyone would do or say anything if they're spotted doing dodgy shit. What's the plan, are we doing a straight shooting so they're all dead, or just bullets in shins, then we get them to the warehouse and kill them there?"

George reared his head back. "They're not dirtying *this* fucking car with their blood. Let's just gun the lot of them down and stuff them in that Transit. I'll drive that to the warehouse, and you can drive this."

"Right." Greg went to get out.

"Hang on. Are you going to be all right with us using the machine guns? The abattoir…"

"I haven't got PTSD if that's what you mean."

"Good."

They both left the car and grabbed gloves and the guns from the boot. George slid his gloves on then stalked across the street and pushed open the diamond-wire gate in the middle of the fencing. It creaked, and he winced, waiting for one of the old boys to come out of the lock-up and start some argy-bargy. He held his finger steady on the trigger, ready.

Nothing happened.

He walked to the door. Ajar. *Fucking plonkers.* He leaned his ear towards it, as did Greg, and listened.

"We're going to kill those creepy twins and be done with it," Dickie said.

"Creepy?" Jordy asked. "More like mad cunts."

George smiled at the mad bit, although he was a tad naffed off at the creepy comment. "*Are* we creepy?" he whispered.

"Shut up," Greg hissed.

"Why kill them?" someone else asked. "What would that achieve? We'd get God knows who else running the estate. Sometimes it's better the devil you know."

"I'll apply to take it over," Dickie said.

Someone laughed.

"Oh, fuck me." Jordy. "Are you off your tree?"

"No, I know a lot about running an estate from Ron. You lot will be my posse."

"The Cardigan Posse?"

"No, the Feathers Posse. I wouldn't keep the estate name. I wonder why the twins did that. I mean, it's not like they took it over from their dad or anything."

George froze. Now *that* kind of speculation could get right in the fucking bin. He shoved the door open and fired in a side-to-side arc. Bodies flew into the air and landed on the floor, blood spraying. It was over in seconds, no satisfaction gained from it like he had when he sawed people up, but it had got the job done quickly, and now they needed to get a shift on in case any residents came barrelling round the corner, alerted by the noise.

"I'll load the bodies," George said. "You're not well enough."

Greg nodded. "I'll concede on that one. You could have given me a chance to shoot some of the wankers, though. I've missed this."

"Sorry, got carried away."

"It was the father comment, wasn't it."

"Yeah. No one needs to hear that nonsense."

George got on with hefting the bodies up and throwing them in the Transit, finding the van keys in a ginger bloke's pocket. He took a rag and a petrol can from the BMW boot. Lighter in his pocket, he returned to the lock-up and doused the rag in petrol. Tipped some just inside the door until it crept to a cardboard box and soaked in. He lit the rag. Threw it in. A whoosh went up, and the nearby cardboard box caught alight. He watched it for a while, mesmerised, the flames jumping from box to box around the perimeter and climbing to scoff at the rafters.

George smiled and handed the can and lighter to Greg who strolled over to the BMW and drove away. George followed in the Transit, parking up outside their warehouse.

He had a lot of chopping up in his future, but first, he needed to let Nessa know the score.

GG: HE'S GONE.

NESSA: YOU'RE SHITTING ME.

GG: WHY THE FUCK WOULD I JOKE ABOUT SOMETHING LIKE THAT?

NESSA: THANK YOU.

GG: NEED FUNERAL MONEY FOR APPEARANCE'S SAKE? FAKE BODY IN A COFFIN.

NESSA: CAN DO.

GG: TAKE IT OUT OF THE NOODLE SAFE TOMORROW AND LET ME KNOW HOW MUCH. I'LL PUT IT BACK SO THE ACCOUNTANT DOESN'T THROW A WOBBLY. NOT A WORD TO A SOUL, UNDERSTAND?

NESSA: WHAT DO YOU TAKE ME FOR? YOU DID ME A MASSIVE FAVOUR. I HOPE HE ROTS WITH THE FISHES.

Chapter Seventeen

In an alley opposite the salon, the man had crapped it seeing those two big men. Who were they? Why had they gone between shops then come back out again? They'd sped off in the same direction as the car containing Anna and her baby. She'd been with a bloke. Her boyfriend? No, he doubted that, because the driver had been sitting in a car outside the salon for ages.

That was the only reason I stayed in the alley. He'd have seen me.

Upset his chance to speak to Anna had been prevented, he checked the coast was clear and stepped out. Walked with his hands in his pockets and his head down in case those shops had CCTV that reached to this side of the street.

Miles away inside his head, working out what was the best time to come and see Anna tomorrow, he stopped short at the sound of footsteps. Looked up.

Someone headed towards him in black clothing, staring straight at him.

Chapter Eighteen

*A*nna had made friends with Shania, writing silly
notes the day after she'd arrived. She didn't have
*a friend of her own and wanted one. When Shania had
written back, asking her to phone the police, the bottom
had fallen out of Anna's world. The police? She'd
written another note, and the next time Mummy had*

told her to go down and give Shania a message — about changing the sheets — she'd dropped hers behind a sofa cushion.

WHY DO I NEED TO PHONE THE POLICE?

Over the next week or so, Anna going downstairs to drop off food or toilet rolls or other things Mummy wanted her to deliver, they'd swapped notes. Mummy always waited at the top of the stairs, saying she didn't want to disturb Shania just yet, there was time enough for that later.

What did that mean?

Anna remembered the notes as she'd memorised them, just like she did when Mummy taught her school lessons.

BECAUSE MY MUM DOESN'T KNOW I'M HERE. THEY LOCKED ME UP.
I WANT TO GO HOME. PLEASE HELP ME.

BUT YOU LIVE HERE. YOU PAY RENT.

I DON'T. PLEASE, TELL SOMEONE WHERE I AM!

BUT YOU DON'T TRY TO RUN AWAY WHEN I OPEN
THE DOOR.

I CAN'T. THEY'LL HURT ME.

HURT YOU? THEY WOULDN'T HURT ANYONE.

But a little worm wriggled in her head after that, and she watched Mummy and Daddy. Sometimes, when she hadn't had her special medicine that Uncle Sidney said she needed, she woke up and listened. Tonight, she crept onto the landing. Mummy and Daddy sat in the bedroom that was usually locked. Spying through the gap by the hinges, Anna stared. Why did they need so many tellies on the wall? Five had pictures of the flat on them, and some showed the rest of the house. On one, Shania sat in bed, crying.

"Why am I here?" she shouted, her voice coming out of the speakers on the desk.

Daddy turned the sound down. "You'll find out soon enough."

"Someone's going to notice I'm not at home."

"Probably, but seeing as your mother's still away for work, it won't be for a while. She might report you missing when she gets home, but the trail will be cold by then. You're left to your own devices when she isn't

171

there—she never checks on you, we know that. You hate it because it's like you don't exist. Do you think we did this without covering our backs? Do you think we'd pick someone whose parents actually give a shit? Silly girl."

"I want my mum. Please, I want my mum."

Anna went back to bed, her eyes stinging. She knew how Shania felt. Anna wanted her mum sometimes when she went out and left her here by herself. If anyone knocked on the door, she got scared and cried for Mummy, wishing she hadn't nipped out. It must be horrible for Shania, not being able to see her mother at all.

Anna hid under the covers, wishing she'd had the medicine and hadn't woken up. What should she do? Mummy and Daddy had their phones on them in little pouches at their waists, or in pockets, or a handbag, so she couldn't phone the police. The front and back doors were always locked; she wasn't allowed out by herself, and if she wanted to play in the garden, Mummy went with her. And should she tell someone if it meant her parents would be taken away for being naughty? Would she have to live with Uncle Sid?

Maybe she could go to school then.

She cried, confused and afraid.

Six months had passed without Anna visiting Shania—Mummy had taken over the job after a couple of months. The next time Mummy asked Anna to go downstairs, she'd said if she had to do it, she'd lose the plot. Anna didn't know what that meant.

Mummy came out of the kitchen, giving her a box with the word TAMPONS *on the side. Was that why she was upset? Because Shania needed what was in the box? Anna walked downstairs, unlocked the flat door, stepped inside, and closed the door. Why did Shania just sit there? Why didn't she try to get away?*

Anna dropped her note and the box on the seat. She backed to the door, still puzzled as to why Shania never ran out while the door was unlocked—did she know Mummy waited at the top of the stairs?

Because she said they'd hurt her, remember?

Oh yeah.

The horrible worm wiggled in her belly.

"Mummy said you have to do some washing. You need to change out of your nightie else you'll smell."

"I don't care if I smell."

"Mummy said if you don't do as you're told, she'll be cross—and she's already cross because you need that box. She was crying and everything."

"Tell Mummy she can come down here and tell me herself instead of sending you."

Anna didn't know what else to say. She left, locking the door, suddenly scared at remembering cameras were in the flat. What if her parents had seen her leaving the other notes? What if they'd seen her doing it this time? Would she be locked downstairs with Shania for being naughty? No, they wouldn't do that to her… She was their princess.

The confusion came back again. One side of her knew this was wrong, but the other side couldn't imagine Mummy and Daddy being mean. Eyes stinging, bottom lip wobbling, she climbed the three stairs, then walked along the landing and trudged up the other steps.

Mummy waited there, her hand out for the key. "Good girl. Would you like some ice cream?"

Anna nodded and stepped into the hallway.

Mummy locked the door and pocketed the key.

YOU CAN GO AND SEE YOUR MUMMY SOON.

Beneath the covers of her bed, Shania read the note again. Tears fell. That lovely little girl was going to save her somehow. She ripped the note up, like she'd done with all the others. Scrunching the pieces into her fist, she went into the bathroom, shut the door, and flushed the bits down the toilet. She hoped this room didn't have any cameras, but if it did, she'd have been questioned about the letters already, wouldn't she? They wouldn't still send Anna down if they knew they were communicating. Did that mean the cameras didn't record the footage? That gave her a measure of relief. The idea that the sex games had been stored somewhere had given her a dose of shame to contend with.

When David had first spoken to her through the hidden speakers, his disembodied voice had shit the life out of her. He'd told her the rules, how she'd be hurt if she tried to escape, how they'd go after her mother. While Mum wasn't the best, Shania still loved her, and she had to keep her safe. She'd endured their depraved sexual kinks, had fought them like David had demanded. The only thing she hadn't done was get pregnant. Maybe she couldn't. They'd revealed their use for her two months after leaving her down here with minimal personal visits. They'd conversed through the speakers, and oddly, even though she loathed them, she'd come to look forward to the human contact.

Mum would have reported her missing by now. Were the police out there, searching for her? She imagined them poking in hedgerows and scouting grass verges. Coppers on doorsteps, asking questions. No one would know she was here unless they'd seen her walking down the street, but it hadn't struck her as the kind of estate where folks nosed out of their windows. Posh nobs were private, weren't they, and didn't involve themselves in other people's business.

But what if the police had come here? What if, by some stroke of luck, someone had seen her arriving on the Friday and Saturday nights? Shania's shoulders slumped. David and Valandra were so sophisticated and believable they'd have no trouble convincing a police officer that they hadn't seen her. Look how she'd fallen for their charms. How she'd thought she'd landed on her feet with this job, the couple too nice for words.

She collected the tampons, showered, then returned to the bedroom, getting dressed. She put her nightie and other washing in the machine, making it look like she'd obeyed Valandra. She made the bed and read for a while.

She all but jumped out of her skin when Anna appeared at the bedroom door.

"Mummy's gone to the shops."

Fear pervaded Shania's whole body. "You shouldn't be down here. Don't let her catch you. Go. Hurry up! Go!"

Anna left.

But she didn't lock the door.

Shania stood on the street for the first time in what felt like forever. Panic and exhilaration coursing through her, she debated which way to go—left, towards home, or right, to the fields at the end of this street? She opted for home, or at least in that direction, so she had houses around her. She didn't want to batter on someone's door here, they might know the Flemingtons and alert them that she'd gone to them, asking to use their phone. Not trusting anyone anymore, she ran, bits of sharp tarmac digging into the soles of her feet. She hadn't put her shoes on—she no longer had any as they'd been in the den when she'd been woken up by Valandra shrieking about Anna going missing.

It seemed so long ago now.

She reached the corner and sped around it, catching sight of a car coming towards her, a big boxy type with tinted windows. A Land Rover? She slowed, walking at a normal pace so the driver didn't think her running was something to take notice of. She could wave them down, ask them to stop, get them to take her to a police station, but something told her not to—a deep fear of speaking to someone who might not be on her side. She had to find a phone box, it would be safer that way, or just keep going until she reached home.

The vehicle passed, and she relaxed. Until she had the horrible thought that it might have been Valandra coming back from the shops. She'd seen David's Porsche on the drive when she'd come to babysit, but what did Valandra drive? But wouldn't she have stopped immediately, got out, and dragged Shania into her car? No, no, she couldn't risk being seen doing that—it was daylight.

Shania kept walking until she reached the end of the road, then picked up her pace again, veering into another street. Halfway home, she allowed herself to laugh—she'd done it, she was free, but what about Anna? How would she explain going down to the flat without being told to? Would they smack her, punish her? The idea of that sweet child living with those monsters spurred her on, and she legged it, not stopping until she reached Windermere Gardens. The relief at seeing the familiar houses slammed into her, and she staggered on, to number seventy-eight, lurching up the front path and whacking the door with the heel of her hand. Would Mum be away for work again? So much time had passed, Shania had lost track. Would she even be home? Was it the weekend or a weekday?

She rushed down the side alley and into the back garden. Snatched up the rock. She could have cried at seeing the key there. She slid it in the lock, turned it, but it seemed the door was already open. She burst inside.

"Mum? Mum? Are you in?"

She lunged for the hallway, where the phone was kept on a tall table. Eyes blurry from tears, she blindly went towards the shape in front of her. Mum's silhouette where she stood by the front door, the sun coming through the glass behind her.

"You didn't really think you'd get away, did you?" a man said.

She blinked. Cleared her vision. Recognised the voice. Oh God. Oh no…

"Valandra gave me a little call, said she'd seen you running. I thought I'd wait here to save my brother the job of leaving work to collect you. He's going to be so angry with you, but then you already know that, don't you."

She spun towards the kitchen, stumbling forward in her haste. Sidney, that horrible man who watched them have sex from the corner, grabbed her hair and wrenched her to a stop.

"Pack it in," he said. "It's pointless trying to get away. Now then, as Mummy's off in Scotland again, we're going to sit down and wait until it gets dark. Then we're going back, understand?"

She closed her eyes. Nodded. But she had the advantage here. She knew where everything was and could use things as a weapon. She could fight him, knock him out, go round to a neighbour.

Anna had given her this chance, and she wasn't going to waste it.

Shania sat in the flat, her wrists sore from where Sidney had tied her up at home. He'd injected her with something, of course he fucking had, and she'd been transported here unconscious. She worried about Anna. The poor girl didn't deserve to be punished for helping her. She'd done what she'd thought was right.

Shania kicked herself. She should have taken the chance and knocked on one of the neighbour's doors. Should have gone into the corner shop she'd passed when escaping. But her fear of her captors had put doubt in her head, erasing her trust in her own thoughts.

She'd never get away now.

She got up and took a notepad out of the kitchen drawer, along with a biro. She wasn't the first, and she doubted she'd be the last, especially as she hadn't given them what they wanted. Another child. Someone else would take her place when it became clear they were flogging a dead horse with her.

If she couldn't save herself, she could at least warn the next girl of what to expect. Whoever it was wouldn't have such a shock, then.

She took a deep breath and put pen to paper.

Dear Someone Like Me…

Chapter Nineteen

"What the feck are ye doin' out here at this time of night?" Ichabod had been appraised of the goings-on via WhatsApp and, knowing the score and what was expected of him, he wanted to get on with it. He'd seen George and Greg leaving from his hiding place—he'd arrived on foot not long before Will had driven Anna away—and the target had stepped farther back into the alley, likely fearful that two brick shithouses had been in the vicinity.

It was so easy to frighten someone when they weren't expecting to see you, like Ichabod had just done to this fella me lad. A quick loom out of the darkness between lampposts, catching him off guard, and Bob's your uncle. *This* prick, though… A nasty piece of work by all accounts. Bastard, George had called him when he'd given Ichabod the specs for this job, as if that were his name, as if he deserved no other.

Bastard's eyes narrowed. Was he contemplating whether to answer the stranger in front of him? Had prison made him wary enough to know this wasn't your usual 'bump into a bloke in the street' kind of thing? Or did he think he'd met a drunkard and could easily scoot past and be on his way?

He seemed to come to a decision. "I've been to the pub."

Liar. "Do ye always hang about in alleys on ye way home, then?" A little nudge to let him know he'd been watched. A nice touch, that, even if Ichabod did say so himself.

"Have you been spying on me?"

"Might have. So come on, what were ye doin' in the alley? I heard a lot of bangin', reckon someone was after thieving one of the shops. Are ye a lookout?"

"No! I needed a piss, that's *all*."

"Ye're lyin' tae me, so ye are."

"I'm not!" Bastard darted his eyes left then right. He must have spotted he couldn't dash between parked cars and run because he stood by the passenger door of one. "Can you let me past, please?"

Ichabod considered toying with him—stepping to the right when Bastard did, blocking his way, then stepping to the left to repeat the process, messing with his head—but he couldn't be arsed. With the twins busy and Ichabod being instructed to apprehend Bastard and meet Janine, he needed to stay on track.

"Ah, ye're not goin' anywhere except wid me."

"What?"

"I said, ye're comin' wid me. Don't even think of feckin' me about. I'm Ichabod by the way. I'd say it's nice tae meet ye, but it isn't, so I won't."

Panic infused Bastard's face. "Look, I don't want any trouble."

"Yet ye've plonked yeself slap bang in the middle of it."

"I don't know what you mean."

"Prowlin', spyin' on Anna. Starin' at her like some perv. I think ye know *full well* what I mean."

"How…how do *you* know her?"

"I don't."

Bastard frowned. "Then why…?"

"Why am I here? Ye'll find out soon enough."

Ichabod gripped Bastard's wrist and squeezed. One wrong move, and he'd break it inside two seconds. It paid to have ninja skills.

He marched the bloke down the street and around to the next where he'd been told to go, Bastard trying to pull his arm free and spluttering that this was "absurd" and "you can't do this to me."

"I can do what I feckin' like, the same as *ye* did what *ye* feckin' liked. I know enough about ye tae understand ye name suits ye—Bastard!"

"That's not my name! You've got me mixed up with someone else."

"Believe me, I haven't."

Ichabod scanned the row of cars at the kerb. Headlights came to life and flashed. Dwayne, the twins' car thief, got out of a vehicle.

"Did ye bring the cuffs?" Ichabod asked quietly.

"Cuffs?" Bastard spluttered.

"Shut ye face," Ichabod warned, idly wondering why the man didn't shout, seeing as they were in a residential street. Maybe prison had taught him to assess situations and twig when it was a lost cause. But where was his fighting spirit, his self-preservation?

"Yeah." Dwayne threw them over the car roof.

Ichabod caught them. "Help me wid this wanker."

Dwayne came round and wrenched Bastard's hands behind his back, forcing him against the stolen car.

"Is this necessary?" Bastard asked.

"I wouldn't be doin' it if it wasn't, ye prick." Ichabod snapped on the cuffs and said in his ear, "Do ye know who The Brothers are? Nah, ye probably don't, not yet, unless ye asked where Ron Cardigan was to get reacquainted with what's what around here."

"I don't know any brothers."

"Right, well, they run the estate. I'm sure ye recall what that is. Ron's dead, and if ye thought *he* was bad, then ye haven't seen anythin' yet."

"I had nothing to do with leaders. I don't agree with dictatorship."

Ichabod laughed. *"Really* now? After what ye were involved in? Feck the feck off, then feck off again."

He opened the back door and shoved Bastard inside, getting in with him. If he gave him any hassle, he'd elbow him in the face and break his nose. Dwayne got in the driver's seat and stared in the rearview, his eyes crinkling, his shoulders shaking with laughter.

"Look, what's going on?" Bastard asked, clearly going down the 'I don't know why I'm here' route.

"I've told ye. Anna. Now shut the feck up."

"She went off with a man. Is she okay?"

Dwayne eased away from the kerb.

"Are ye *really* concerned that someone's abducted her? Or just pissed of ye didn't get tae her first?"

Bastard flinched in the light of a streetlamp flashing on his features.

Have I hit a nerve with that? Why does abduction bother him so much?

"Of course I'm concerned!" Bastard said, affronted. "I want to keep her with me, and if someone's taken her off—"

"They have, tae keep her safe from the likes of ye. And like I said, shut the feck up."

The journey to The Moon Estate was spent with Bastard nattering on regardless of the warning, Ichabod and Dwayne ignoring him. Bastard had pleaded his case: he loved Anna, wanted to keep her hidden; he'd thought about her for years, couldn't get her out of his head; he wanted to smother her son.

"Ye what? *Smother*?" Ichabod said, unable to keep quiet any longer.

"You wouldn't understand."

"Look, ye're comin' off as a freak, so I'd zip it if I were ye. All ye've said is up here." Ichabod tapped his head. "Ready for me tae pass on. Ye sound a psycho, and it won't do ye any favours where we're goin'." He glanced out of the window. "Ah, we're here."

Dwayne had pulled up onto the driveway of a house. Bacon, one of Moon's men, lived here, although he didn't come out to see what was going on. Moon had likely warned him someone would be coming to use the air-raid shelter in the back garden. The twins had arranged for the tête à tête to be here, because taking Bastard to the warehouse when they'd be sawing up bodies meant the man wouldn't get undivided attention, and he needed to be questioned in a calm environment so they could extract as much information out of him as possible.

Following this monster had pulled Ichabod away from his job at the casino, but he'd never say no to The Brothers. Jackpot Palace was in capable hands, so nothing to worry about there. Anyway, he enjoyed these little forays into the dark side, they gave him a chance to flex the evil streak in his DNA.

He got out and dragged Bastard from the car. Dwayne reversed, likely to dump the car and burn it out. Ichabod marched his quarry down the side of the house and into the back garden. A light snapped on, coming through one of the lower windows.

Bastard glanced around, again not screaming for help. Other houses stood nearby, so why wasn't he trying to get someone's attention? Was he that warped, he thought Ichabod would relent and take him to Anna? That if he behaved like a good little boy, he'd get what he wanted? Was that how he'd behaved in prison and, like a child who'd learned how to play their parents, he repeated that here?

Ichabod manhandled him to the window. Bacon stood there, and he nodded, then switched the light off.

Bastard sucked in a breath. "Please, I don't understand why I'm here… Why are you doing this to me?"

"Oh, bore off." Ichabod took him down the steps into the shelter.

Bastard stumbled all the way, desperately trying to right his footing. Darkness engulfed the place apart from a harsh spotlight trained on a chair in the centre, and Ichabod marched him over there, digging his fingertips into the softness of his upper arm.

"Sit." He pushed him down, hoping the cuffs bit into him as they pressed against the back of the chair.

Bastard blinked at the light.

"Why didn't ye try to get away or scream?" Ichabod asked,

"Because you might know where Anna is. You might help me find her."

"I'd never tell ye where she is."

"Are you in with the man who took her?"

"Yes."

"Oh God, this can't be happening again."

Annoyed, Ichabod frowned. "What are ye talkin' about?"

"An abduction. Oh shit, are you involved with *him*?"

"Who?"

"The one who did it before."

What the chuff is he bangin' on about? "Listen tae me, ye prick. Whatever ye're sayin', I'm not interested. All I want tae do is my job, so be quiet until the police get here."

"The police? What? I mean…why have you called *them*? I haven't done anything! I just want to take Anna away."

"Can ye hear yeself, how weird ye sound?"

Something wasn't right here. Bastard acted as if it was *okay* to take Anna and smother Harper. It was obvious now that he had a mental health issue.

Footsteps tapped on the stairs, and Ichabod glanced over into the darkness. A shape emerged the closer the figure got to the edge of the corona of light. Janine. She remained in the half-shadows, staring at Bastard.

Ichabod went to her and whispered, "He's said some strange stuff, as if he wants to abduct Anna—and he definitely said he wants tae smother Harper. Yet he's panicked about someone else abductin' her. I'm concerned for the state of his mind, so I am. All these things he's sayin', I don't get it."

"I do. You can go up and see Cameron if you don't want to be here. He's parked out the front."

"Nah, I'll sit on the stairs in case *he* turns on ye."

"He won't be able to. Moon got hold of me. Said there's rope on a sideboard." She switched on her phone and accessed the torch app.

"Who else is there?" Bastard asked, his voice wavering. "What are you whispering about?"

They ignored him. Janine swept the beam around in the murky area opposite the chair, found the sideboard, and walked over. She came back to Ichabod and handed him the rope, then she switched her torch off and returned to the sideboard. She'd have the perfect vantage point to question the man from there but remain hidden. It would be more frightening that way, Bastard unable to see her.

Ichabod approached him, the man's eyes widening in fear.

"Please, don't hurt me…"

"I'm just tyin' ye tae the feckin' chair so my friend here can speak tae ye." He roped him up then moved to sit on the stairs and listen, calling to Janine, "The floor's all yours."

Chapter Twenty

Nessa sat in her flat above the Noodle and again counted the five grand she'd taken from the safe. Thank God the twins were paying for this, because she didn't want to have to fork out some of her savings on her father. The twins paid her a lot of money to run the pub. Her food and drink came with the job, as did the utility bills, so she'd been able to pop a fair bit in her personal safe—sod using a bank and letting any go to the taxman. People would assume George and Greg handled that anyway, and she wouldn't disabuse them of the situation by telling them she was classed as self-employed.

She'd hold the wake here, get the chef to prepare a buffet, finger foods and sandwiches, cheese and pineapple on sticks, all those things Dad would have eaten at parties in his youth, a right old-fashioned spread. There'd be a ska band, too. It was what his cronies would expect—if any of them were still alive. She imagined they'd been killed, too, but they'd be classed as 'missing'.

The twins shelling out for the funeral wasn't unusual, they'd done it countless times before for others, but without a body, things were going to be…interesting. She assumed they'd pay someone to cover it up, filling the coffin with bricks to match Dad's weight, but who'd be left to deal with Mum wondering why she couldn't see her husband one last time?

Me, for fuck's sake.

Perhaps a small price to pay for not having Dickie Feathers in her life anymore.

It would probably be a cremation. Bribing a church official wouldn't be an easy sway, but then again, George and Greg had fingers in many pies, so maybe they'd pull it off. It wasn't her problem. They'd killed someone prominent, it'd be noticed if Dad wasn't around, and people wouldn't believe he'd just disappeared with his mates. The charade had to be endured, and Nessa would fake cry throughout the service so suspicions weren't aroused.

Her phone blipped, and she grabbed it.

GG: BE PREPARED TO GET A CALL FROM YOUR OLD DEAR. A PRIVATE CLINIC'S GETTING HOLD OF HER TO SAY HE'S BEEN IN A CAR ACCIDENT. THEY'LL LET HER KNOW HE'S TOO BASHED UP FOR HER TO GO AND IDENTIFY HIM, SO THEY'LL DO IT THROUGH DNA. YOU'LL DEAL WITH THAT FOR HER, I DON'T WANT HER ANYWHERE NEAR THAT CLINIC. PROMPT HER TO GIVE YOU HIS TOOTHBRUSH.

NESSA: HOW LONG HAVE I GOT BEFORE SHE RINGS?

GG: THEY'RE CONTACTING HER AS WE SPEAK. WE'LL GET ON TO THE CREM TOMORROW. BEEN A BIT BUSY SO NEED SOME KIP. DELETE THESE MESSAGES.

NESSA: OKAY.

She erased the conversation and stood, taking a deep breath.

Her phone trilled, and she stared at the screen. *Here we go…*

She swiped to answer. "Hello? Mum? Why are you ringing in the middle of the night? Is everything okay?"

A snort piped down the line. Nessa had expected a dramatic wail.

"Mum? What's wrong?"

"I've…I've just had a phone call from a private clinic."

"Is it Dad?" The logical conclusion to come to and something Mum would expect her to say.

"Yes. He's dead."

"What?"

"Dead. Car accident."

"Oh no. Oh God." *Why isn't she crying?* "How come he's in a private clinic? Why isn't he in hospital?"

"The man said the twins had given him private healthcare when he retired, but…but he didn't tell me that when I had my breast lump, the selfish prick! I had to wait for the NHS."

Prick? Her attitude's changed. "Maybe it only extended to him. Listen, I'm coming over, okay?

We'll go and see him together. I don't want you doing this on your own."

"I can't go," Mum said. "The man said…he said he hasn't got a face anymore. The lamppost your father drove into caved it in."

"Oh, bloody hell… I'm so sorry." *I'm not.* "Do you want me to stay on the phone while I drive round?"

"If you want to."

Frowning at Mum's response and how she wasn't in hysterics, Nessa went downstairs, set the alarm, and walked out the back to her car. She put the phone and her handbag on the passenger seat, speaker on. "You still there?"

Silence answered her.

"I'm on my way now, all right?"

She drove through the streets, in no hurry. Mum wasn't going anywhere, and the woman had never shown any urgency when Nessa had problems, so she wouldn't give her the nice treatment. Some would say she was wicked for being like this, but her apathy towards Mum had only increased as she'd got older, her resentment doubling year on year until it filled her so much she thought she'd burst with it.

She parked outside the house—only Mum's now—and grabbed her phone. "I'm here. I've got my key."

She cut the call and let herself in, finding Mum in the living room. Phone slipped into her bag, she assessed the situation. No tears. No red eyes.

"It's been a long forty-two years," Mum said.

Nessa could imagine. It had been a long forty years for herself.

"He bullied me the whole time, you know," Mum said, as if Nessa didn't have eyes and ears and hadn't seen it all for herself. "I bet he was with that Marlborough bitch. I hope she's dead as well. They've been carrying on for years. He said he ended it, but he didn't. I swear one of her kids is his."

Nessa sat on an armchair—or rather thudded onto it. "What?"

"He looks like him, that Chesney. And what kind of name is *that*?"

"How old is he?"

"Eighteen."

Nessa tried to wrap her head around the age thing. "Is the Marlborough woman younger than Dad or something?"

"Hmm, by twenty years. She was thirty when she had the kid, she's forty-eight now."

"Did you ever say anything about the baby?"

"Yes, and he slapped me, told me not to spout bullshit."

That sounded about right.

Mum's stare turned steely. "I'm going to sign this house over to you. I don't want that Chesney or his mother getting their grubby hands on it when I'm dead. The Marlboroughs are a greedy lot, always have been, that's why they're so loaded. He'll make a claim if I don't get things in order."

"But you don't even know for sure whether he's Dad's son."

Mum glared at her. "Do you want to take the chance? Have some skinny little posh twat taking away half of your inheritance?"

"Not really," Nessa lied. Privately, she thought Chesney deserved half the proceeds from the sale if he'd grown up with a father like Dickie. Or had Dad treated him differently because he was a boy? *Probably.*

"I put up with a lot from your father, I was meek because he made me that way, but I don't have to do that anymore. I may be sixty-eight, but

I've got a lot of life to catch up on." Mum sagged as though all the tension Dad had sewn into her over the years had just unravelled.

Nessa still didn't feel sorry for her, and that was sad, because maybe she should. *But think about how she treated you. She doesn't deserve your sympathy.* "I'll handle the funeral, okay? You leave everything to me."

"Right. I don't have access to the bank account anyway. He never let me have a cheque book or card."

Nessa remember it well, how Dad controlled the purse strings. "Is there any cash lying about?"

"Yes, in the safe upstairs, so I'll be all right."

"I'll make a cuppa, shall I?"

Mum nodded. "Do me a favour and ask those twins if someone else was in the car with him. Ask if *that woman's* dead an' all. I bet he took her to a flashy restaurant Up West, had too much to drink, and crashed on the way home."

"I'll phone them in a minute."

Nessa left the room and went into the kitchen, shutting the door. She didn't phone, instead having a one-sided conversation with herself, loudly, in case Mum was listening. She'd think Nessa had done as she was told, but she didn't intend on doing that ever again once the funeral was over. She'd be there for Mum for appearance's sake at the crem and the wake, but after that, she'd keep her distance.

Tea made, she returned to the living room and put Mum's cup on the little table by the sofa. "She wasn't with him." She sat and blew on her tea.

"Oh. Well…" Mum shrugged. "Shame. I'd hoped she'd be dead. Now I've still got to see her down the market."

"Not if you move away, start again." A selfish but necessary suggestion—the less Nessa had to do with Mum, the better her life would be. The love for her parents had waned significantly as the years had gone by, and now all she had left was a kernel on the cusp of shrivelling to a husk.

Mum's eyes lit up. "Not a bad idea. I could sell up, still transfer the new house to your name. I'll do that after I've got the death certificate. Attending that funeral is the last thing I'll do for that bastard of a man."

So she'd faked her devotion for Dad all this time? Had settled for her lot and played the part? Nessa had never seen this side of her mother. What had Dad said to her to make Mum so afraid that she didn't have the courage to leave him?

Nessa didn't think for one second she'd stuck around for her. So what had happened?

"He always held it over me," Mum said quietly. She gazed at the carpet, a million miles away.

"Held what?"

"That I didn't have a son."

"He did it to me, too."

"Hmm. *And* because I helped your nan get away from Grandad."

Nessa searched her memories. "Nanny Feathers?"

"Hmm. *He* was a bastard an' all, your gramps. Used to beat her regularly—probably where Dickie got the idea from, he'd seen it growing up."

"What went on back then?"

"I kept her savings pot here and gave it to her when she had enough to run. I was going to join Nanny Feathers a few months later, but your dad found out. He said he'd kill me if I ever tried to do the same. Said Ron had forbidden me from leaving London."

"What's it got to do with Ron where you lived?"

"You have to understand that Ron was a different breed to the twins. If he said you stayed, you stayed. If you left, he'd find you. Kill you. Dickie was one of his top men, he'd have wanted to keep him sweet."

"But you could have left once the twins took over. They'd have helped you."

Mum's mouth skewed. "By then, I didn't *want* to leave. I wasn't going to let his fancy piece have him all to herself. He was mine long before he was hers."

Nessa didn't get her way of thinking. If you hated your life, you got out as soon as you could. Why stay with a wanker who treated you like that just to spite his mistress?

She's not right in the head.

The little girl inside Nessa wanted an answer to a particular question, but she dreaded the response because she already knew what it was. Still, hope bloomed whether or not there was water to nourish it, a weed that never gave up. "Would you have taken me with you?"

Mum's eyebrows shot up, and she chuffed out a mean laugh. "Why would I do *that*? I never wanted you in the first bloody place. I didn't want *any* kids once I realised what Dickie was like. One year of marriage to him, and he showed me all I needed to know. But by then, it was too late. I was stuck."

The spear of hurt that should have wounded Nessa missed its mark. She'd always known Mum hadn't loved her, and having it confirmed was thankfully a release, not painful, permission for her to relinquish any duty she'd felt towards the woman. And Mum saying after a year it was too late, was that true?

I don't believe her.

And her mother was only giving her the house out of spite, because she didn't want Chesney to have it.

Maybe I'll pay the Marlboroughs a visit when Mum's snuffed it. Get a DNA test done.

She stared at her mother who'd closed her eyes.

And I'll give that kid half the house.

She smiled to herself. Retribution, although Mum wouldn't know about it when it happened, was a sweet, sweet thing.

Chapter Twenty-One

*D*ays *and days had passed. Anna hadn't come down to deliver any notes, she hadn't brought any shopping like she had with Shania. Sidney had done it. So the girl was being kept away. Did that mean Anna had tried to help Shania escape? Didn't they trust her anymore?*

David had spoken to Rusty through hidden speakers, mainly in what she assumed was the evenings. She'd spent her days inside her head until Sidney had brought her a cardboard box of books. Romances, not her thing, but she'd been grateful for something to take away the monotony.

Sitting there inspecting her life before she'd come here hadn't been pleasant. She'd had to face every ugly scar on her psyche, see her mother and father for exactly who they were—and herself. She could now admit she was a selfish person, wanting only what was best for her. She'd chosen to go to university so she didn't have the burden of responsibility anymore— she'd been prepared to let Mum go to the dogs in order to save her own sanity. Not such a bad thing, mental well-being was important, and it wasn't her job to police her mother.

She still struggled with that mindset.

When quite a few marks had been scored into the painted wood to keep track of time, her true experience of who they really were had been revealed. She was still sore between her legs from last night's rape— David had used her brutally, Valandra slapping and biting her while he'd committed such a terrible sin, Sidney sitting in the corner of the bedroom, playing with himself. The degradation had been the ultimate shame, and she'd hated herself for fighting them when it was clear that's what they wanted her to do. But *she'd do* whatever *they asked of her. It served her purpose.*

Their reason for leaving her for two months by herself? To work out when she'd be most fertile. For her to ask for tampons. She'd had a period shortly after arriving, then another, and their first visit was the ideal time for her to conceive. She didn't tell them she'd had a coil fitted to help with her painful periods. Why give them a chance to kill her now? She'd bought herself some time. How long would they give her, though? How many failed attempts would they allow?

More nicks had been carved into the wood.

She'd endured many nights of their disgusting pawing, them tying her up, whipping her, suffocating her to the point of going unconscious then reviving her to do it all over again. She'd quickly learned to block out what they were doing, even the pain to some degree, although the aftermath of that had her hobbling during the day.

Now, on the seventieth day of her being here, they hadn't come down at night. Were they waiting to see if she was pregnant? How would they react when her period came again?

She curled into a ball on her bed and closed her eyes, then snapped them open, forcing herself to remain awake. If she slept, she'd lose track of whether it was day or night. Then she remembered she'd be able to work out which day it was when she came on, she was regular, but still, this was the only control she had, marking off each day, sticking to rigid times of being awake, and she wanted to hold on to it.

Hunger took her to the kitchen. This morning, Sidney had brought some eggs, cheese, and mushrooms, suggesting she make an omelette as the protein would do her good. She'd do as he'd said — but only because she wanted them to think she'd do whatever they wanted. She played the long game, and one day, she'd get out of here.

She wouldn't be Lacey or Shania, dying in this place.

Valandra thought back to Shania and how she'd had period after period. Would the same happen with Rusty? Three years ago, she'd told David they should take someone sooner, when Anna had been five, but he hadn't been ready to have another child then. When he was, Shania had come into the picture and ruined things. Now there was Rusty to pin his hopes on, and he'd raged earlier that if she didn't produce the goods, he'd kill her sooner than Shania and move on to *someone else—someone he'd already vetted for this eventuality. He'd ranted as if Rusty's reproductive system, if it was defective, was Valandra's fault. He'd become slightly unhinged, frightening her, giving her pause to question once more who he really was and whether he'd been hiding a part of himself from her. She'd been about to broach the subject of Anna going to school again, but stupidity wasn't her middle name, and she'd kept it to herself, listening to him rail, agreeing to pacify him.*

Since Anna had forgotten to lock the flat door, enabling Shania to escape, David had been even stricter with what she could do indoors and when Valandra could take her on little trips. Her fun days out had been restricted to once a month as punishment since the Shania debacle, which limited Valandra being able to teach her things. She was supposed to have been to the history museum by now, it was on the syllabus, and Valandra had to give her a virtual tour online so Anna could do a project about it and send it in.

David didn't understand the pressure of homeschooling her, how Valandra had to ensure Anna learned all the things on the list. It wasn't a case of picking or choosing, she had to teach her these subjects. Add to that the way she had to watch the child extra carefully in case she found the new hiding place for the spare key and crept down to Rusty, not to mention the months after Shania's death where Valandra had been paranoid that the woman had poisoned Anna's mind and given her the idea of escaping herself.

It wasn't fair for David to impose these things on Valandra when he swanned off to work, free of the responsibility. For the first time, she wanted to shout, "She isn't even my child! You sort her out!" Now, she had doubts regarding his love for her. There was the option of leaving him, but she couldn't even if she wanted to. She'd been complicit in everything, and he had the video evidence to prove it. Besides, he'd find her—with his contacts, she had no chance of remaining undetected, and she didn't know anyone who'd give her a new passport, driving licence, and birth certificate with a new name.

She frowned at her thoughts. How silly of her to contemplate walking away. How mad to entertain striking a match and setting this house on fire, taking Anna with her, leaving David and Sidney inside. Doing it twice in one lifetime was utterly stupid. She'd got away with it before by hiding out in one of the farm fields, tending to the sheep her alibi, then returning home to find the house fully ablaze, a fire crew and the police there, parents burned to a crisp.

No one would believe her if she did it again.

But it frightened her that it had crossed her mind, that she'd come to a sticking point in her life for the second time, which forced her to imagine such things. She might be able to come and go as she pleased here, but even though she wasn't a caged bird as such, she was *trapped.*

Sidney came over whenever she needed a sitter as he'd reduced his working hours. She'd often left Anna alone in between Shania and Rusty living here so she could breathe*. This life had the strains of her childhood running through it, her every move orchestrated, her thoughts channelled to match the people who conducted her days—David and Sidney, always there to remind her that they'd saved her, put her on the path to stardom, and gave her everything she wanted. She'd been too blind to see she'd walked from one form of incarceration into another.*

Why then, did she feel it was okay to lock women up downstairs? A therapist would be able to unpick her reasons, but she suspected she wanted to understand how her parents had felt while ruling over her, to feel their power, to be the one in control.

Lately, she'd come to realise her days were governed by two men's stipulations and rules—ones she no longer agreed with, especially when it came to Anna.

She loved that child, wanted the best for her, and cooping her up in here wasn't the way to go. Valandra may be one of the worst bitches to ever walk this planet, but she wanted more for Anna. What if that poor girl's mind warped like hers had? What if she left this house as an adult who wasn't quite…stable? They were no better than Valandra's parents. She'd become her own mother, and he'd become her father, ruling the child.

She shuddered. Took a deep breath. Removed his cup from beneath the spout on the posh coffee maker and carried it up to the observation room. He'd received some news today, which he wanted to give to Rusty—he felt her knowing would ensure she continued to do as she was told. At least he'd agreed for Valandra to be there in case the woman became hysterical.

Once again, it had been made all too clear that Valandra was a convenient ally, one he used when he needed to. And that perhaps, if she allowed herself to really admit it, he only needed her as a pretend mother, someone to parade around with her fake pregnancy belly so his secret was safe.

Had David and Sidney chosen her to be their plaything, the same as the mothers-to-be had been chosen, only they dressed it up as so much more?

She swallowed tightly at the thought. How unpleasant to start questioning your purpose. It could only lead to disturbing things if she continued to let her mind roam.

"I have something to tell you, Slave," David said through the speakers.

Rusty stared in the general direction his voice had come from. Where were the speakers? They'd been hidden well. Her stomach rolled over, despite her telling herself his news would be more of the same shit she'd already heard—if you don't get pregnant, you'll pay; if you don't do as we say, you'll pay; if you…if you…if you…

She braced herself.

"Your mother's in hospital." He'd delivered it with no emotion.

Rusty didn't know what to say. Why was she in hospital? Had they put her there? Had Rusty done something wrong and they'd hurt her to prove a point? Or was it the drink? Did David want her to ask those questions? To see her reaction? She'd schooled her features already, wouldn't give him the satisfaction of knowing he'd worried her, but she might not be so clever with her voice. It could wobble. Betray her.

"One vodka too many, so I heard," he said, nonchalant. "She had to have her stomach pumped. Let's see if I'm right: What sent her diving headfirst into a bottle?"

"My father." She had to give him something. While he generally sounded affable when they spoke, she'd quickly learned that not interacting, if he clearly wanted her to, earned her more whip strikes.

"Oh. I'd guessed as much. Some women can't function without a man. I'll let you know if she dies, of course I will, although obviously you won't be going to her funeral."

She waited for him to say more, but only silence surrounded her, the air buzzing with it. She remained on the bed, staring at the wall, focusing on what Valandra had told her yesterday so she didn't get upset about Mum. The photographs she'd taken of her the other evening had all sold out. Who had them framed and on their walls? Who walked past them and stared at her body parts? Who would, given time, be so used to them being there that they barely cast her a glance?

Who would forget her, like everyone else in her life must have?

She woke to the sound of whispers. Disorientated and groggy from sleep, she cracked her eyes open and looked around the bedroom. It felt like the middle of the night, but maybe she'd slept extra-hard and it was morning.

"Rusty…"

She stared at the chandelier where she thought the camera was.

"I'm going to help you," Valandra said.

"What?" Was this a trick? Another of their mad games?

"He's asleep, but I'll have to be quick in case he wakes up. I can get you out of here, but there are conditions."

"I'm not stupid enough to walk into a trap."

"I promise, it isn't one. I'll set you free if you do something for me."

"Like what?"

"Kill David and Sidney."

Rusty blinked. Digested that. "Go away. You're playing with me."

"I'm not. I have to get Anna away from them. David isn't healthy for her. He's become more…strange lately." Muffled movement. "I have to

go; I think he's waking up. I'll speak to you again tomorrow."

Rusty sighed, sick of being messed with. Tears welled, and she scrunched her eyes to stop them from falling. Valandra would lure her into a false sense of security, and just when Rusty took the dangled carrot, they'd strike.

No, she didn't trust that woman. She'd get out of here somehow on her own.

Chapter Twenty-Two

Janine stared at the man who no longer resembled the mugshot in the police file. The resemblance was still there, to who he'd once been, but prison had given him a haunted look, hollows beneath his eyes, deep wrinkles beside them. A thick scar ruined his cheek, and she recalled how he'd got it. Whoever had sewn it up hadn't done as good a job as the nurse had with Faith Lemon's Cheshire.

The whimsical thought came that if things had been different, she wouldn't be standing here today. If Bastard hadn't chosen such a wicked path, he wouldn't be here either. If life was preordained by fate like some believed, then God wasn't a kind and giving being if He let it all go ahead exactly as it had been mapped out. The evils Bastard had committed—how could God even allow those on his destined map in the first place? Or was it choice that had brought them here today? Was it as others said, that humans made their own destinies?

"What happened to you, to make you do what you did?" she asked, flexing her gloved fingers. She knew, but she wanted him in a particular state of mind. As someone well-versed in interviewing criminals, she'd had a lot of practice in drawing pictures in minds with only a few well-chosen words. A hint of something—*what happened to you?*—could bring a whole host of nasty memories to the forefront.

Did his mind fill now, the screen of his thoughts showing a little girl in a cornfield, chasing her puppy who'd slipped the lead?

Mummy and Daddy would be cross if she lost the dog, and she was desperate to get him back. Had the screen faded to black as a man had appeared, his hand outstretched to snatch at the girl's hair? Didn't Bastard want to remember what had happened next? The hands around the throat, choking her. The breath going stale in her lungs. The wheeze as she tried to suck in more air. The hand going up her skirt. The death, then the violation and, the last vile act, the puppy being killed and draped over her lifeless body to be found by Bastard himself.

She hoped he saw it all. Saw it as if he was *right there*, an invisible forcefield preventing him from going to save her, to rewrite the past.

Tears welled in his eyes.

Yeah, you saw it.

"Your childhood, what was it like?" She rested her arse against the sideboard. Studied his expression, now shuttered, the tears gone.

"I don't want to talk about it." He looked down, perhaps at the large spider scuttling across the floor, disappearing into the darkness.

Janine shuddered. *That scream because of a big spider…* Poor Anna, being used in that way.

221

"Well, *I* want to talk about it, so unless you'd like Ichabod to hurt you before I do, then you'll tell me."

He kept his head bent. "A horrible thing happened."

"I know." Now she'd got him thinking about it, she didn't have to push it further.

She wanted all of those *other* memories to come back now: the fear, the desperation, the crushing knowledge that someone he loved was never going home. In short, she wanted him to feel like Lacey, Shania, and Rusty: *they'd* thought they weren't going home either; *they'd* been afraid and desperate, too.

"Did you get the blame for that little girl's murder?" She recalled what had been in his statement. "Silly me, I know you did. Your dad had a heart attack, didn't he, when that girl didn't come home. He died, so not only did you have her death to contend with, you had his on top. And your mother, she blamed you for all of it. If you'd been watching the child like you'd been told to, that man wouldn't have—"

"No more. Please, no more."

"Do you think that's what turned your brain?" she asked. "All of that trauma, too much at once?"

"My brain didn't turn, I've always been like this."

"What, someone willing to let a nonce take a five-year-old away?"

"No, absolutely *not*!"

"What then, a sexual deviant?"

"It's not deviancy. It's pleasure."

"I see. But you *can't* have always been like it because you'd have had no sexual desire as a small boy, but that's splitting hairs... Maybe you meant you've always been a tosser. In that case, I feel for your mother. Maybe she had a reason to blame you. Maybe, because you're such a pervert, you *let* the man take the child so you could watch what he did."

"No! And leave my mother out of this. She was a fucking cow and—" He gritted his teeth, closed his eyes.

"A sore spot, is she?"

He didn't respond.

"I think you killed her. I've had a lot of time to piece things together. She got old, a burden. You couldn't stand her..."

"She deserved it."

"Where did you put her body?"

He stubbornly jutted his jaw.

She'd never been found, nor had Lacey or Shania. Three graves out there, containing women who'd died because they'd hadn't been up to scratch.

Janine tried to feel sorry for the boy he'd been, the burden of guilt placed on his shoulders. But that boy had grown into a hideous man, and any empathy she'd have had for his younger self evaporated in the blaring light of his debauched acts. "Back to the deviancy. I really need to understand. Do you feel there's no harm in it?"

His eyes flashed open. "Of *course* there isn't! What people do in the comfort of their own home is their business."

"Providing all parties consent, yes."

"I'm not discussing that side of it."

"No, because that means facing up to things you'd rather not. I'm curious…aren't you just as bad as the man in the cornfield? He took what wasn't his, too."

"I'm nothing like him," he roared.

Ah, so he doesn't like being compared to him. Doesn't see himself as the same. His mind's broken.

224

She wasn't getting anywhere with this subject. "Why did you employ a private detective to find Anna in Manchester?"

Startled, he blinked in her direction. "How did *you* know about that?"

"I'm a police officer. I got a warrant to look at your bank account."

"That's not right!"

"I assure you it's above board, and even if it wasn't, there's fuck all you can do about it. So answer me: why did you want to find Anna? Why couldn't you just leave her alone?"

"I have to look after her. She isn't safe out there."

Janine knew exactly why he felt this way; his brain had shorted out when the cornfield event had occurred and he'd never been able to function the same again. He believed Anna would be abducted. A therapist would have helped, but he'd never been given the opportunity to talk through it with one. His mother had blocked that avenue.

Maybe that's why he killed her, amongst other things.

She pushed off the sideboard and paced in the murk, arms folded. "Why isn't she safe?"

"People are just waiting to abduct, to kill. I can't let that happen to her."

"Yet you want to abduct her yourself. You want to *smother* her son. Hardly normal behaviour, is it."

"I want to smother him in *protection*! You'll never understand."

"I've read the file, your confession, so I have a good idea of how your mind works. What you don't seem to have grasped is that the 'horrible thing' you mentioned is a rare event. It's unlikely it would have happened to Anna. And besides, she's not a kid anymore, she's not as vulnerable. She has people who are looking after her. She'll never be in any danger, not now. *She doesn't need you*."

"It doesn't just happen to children."

"I know—and as I said, I'm a police officer."

His gaze searched the darkness for her. "Who's that man who took her? Where has she gone?" He gritted his teeth and scrunched his eyes. "I can't *stand* not knowing where she is."

She'd enjoy twisting the knife further. Yes, Ichabod had mentioned he thought Bastard had mental health issues, but honestly, she didn't give a shiny shite. Whether he was unstable or not, she'd treat him like any other healthy offender who needed to pay for his crimes the twins' way—*her* way. The justice system would say he'd already paid by serving his sentence, but in her opinion he'd got off lightly, time spent in jail with no bills to pay, no worries other than getting raped in the shower or shanked by men who hated him for what he'd done. She wished he'd been attacked, maimed, assaulted to within an inch of his life more often, not just a few times when he'd first walked into Belmarsh. But she *couldn't* say she wished he'd never been let out, because if he hadn't, she wouldn't have the pleasure of tormenting him now, fucking with his head, giving him a taste of his own medicine.

Some cases stuck with her more than others. She knew this one inside out, lived and breathed it every time she opened the file to teach other officers about it. It invaded her dreams sometimes, but not as much as it had when she'd first become embroiled in it—back then it had been too shocking to just file away.

"You had many years not knowing where she was while you spent your time in a cell," she reminded him. "No clue who'd infiltrated her life and had control of her. No idea how many times *she went outside*."

"Stop! Stop!"

"Don't you like the idea of her being *outside*?"

"No! It's torture!"

"I doubt it. Not as torturous as what happened to Lacey, Shania, and Rusty. I wonder whether they'd agree with you. Whether they'd say your sexual proclivities were *consensual*. Those young women didn't deserve what happened to them. At least the bad genes didn't extend to Anna. She tried to help Shania. She knew it was wrong. That poor girl *knew* women were being held in that flat, and you don't seem to have any remorse that she was damaged by it. All you're interested in is taking her and Harper."

"They belong with me." He rocked, the front chair legs rising then smacking down. "I have to keep them safe, have to keep them safe, have to—"

"*Shut up!*" she shouted, her neck cords straining. "You don't get to breathe the same air as her unless she says it's okay. You don't get to call the shots anymore. It's no longer your call to make. And I bet that stings, doesn't it? That you're not the one making the rules?"

"Please, I just need to find her."

Janine ploughed on. "Do you think about Rusty and wonder where she is now? Do you ask yourself whether she had a baby and it's allowed *outside*?"

She walked in the darkness and halted behind the chair. Took a pair of pruning shears from her back pocket and knelt. Stared at his hands poking out from the lowest rung of the ladderback.

"What are you doing?" Bastard whispered.

"Jaysus fuckin' wept," Ichabod muttered. "Never thought I'd see the day."

Janine glanced over at the Irishman. "I might be a copper, but I've got scores to settle like everyone else. I'm human. I think bad things. I wish ill on people. You can be nice as pie and still hope someone dies. That case has haunted me for a long time, and I've dreamt of this day like you wouldn't believe."

She faced Bastard's hands again. Gripped a pinkie finger. Positioned the shears.

"Oh God, please, no…" Bastard's breathing quickened.

"There's a special place in Hell reserved for people like you," she said.

Snip.

He screamed, drumming his feet on the floor. Blood dripped, and Janine stared, counting each drop, imagining them as the seconds of a clock ticking by in that flat, the days seeming endless, the nights even longer when that evil trio came in and did whatever the hell they wanted, one a silent observer in the corner until he issued demands, new ideas, revving the other two up, adding to the women's agony and revelling in their cries, their tears.

Snip.

Snip.

Snip.

Just the thumb left on that hand. If it was anything like the pointer and middle fingers, she'd have to put some effort into it again as they'd been tough to cut and her hand had cramped. She stood, deciding not to bother. He screamed so much she needed to get away from him. Backing into the darkness, she threw the shears into a corner and walked towards the stairs. Took her phone out and switched the torch on, shining it at Ichabod.

"I need some air, away from that filthy bastard."

He stood and let her go first, his footsteps tapping behind her. Out in the open, she sucked in a deep breath and stared at the sky, no regrets for what she'd done down there. Still, tears fell down her cheeks.

Ichabod came to stand beside her. "What the feckin' hell is he on?"

"His sister was abducted as a little girl. Murdered. It's twisted his brain."

"That's…a tough one for anyone tae get over."

"It is, but thousands of people have had this happen and they don't behave like him. I understand it, he doesn't want Anna to get abducted, but I think his mind's stuck in the past and he sees her as a girl, even though he knows she's a woman, make sense? There's probably a name for it, like it's a phenomenon, but I have no idea what it is."

"Where's Janet when ye need her tae explain things," Ichabod muttered.

Janine laughed. "Dead, like he will be, and good fucking riddance."

"Those women ye mentioned. What happened tae them?"

She told him the abridged version.

"Any reason why ye cut his fingers off?"

"No, I just wanted to hurt him."

"Any reason why this affects ye more than it possibly should?"

She shone the light on the grass. A daddy longlegs sprang away in alarm. "You could say that." She sighed.

"Why's that, then?"

She closed her eyes. "Because I'm Rusty."

"*What*? Oh, ye poor cow." He laid a hand on her shoulder.

She allowed it.

"So ye mammy…?"

"I chose not to tell her about the babysitting job. Then again, if she'd been a normal parent, I wouldn't have had to hide it." She went on tell him what she'd been through on that score. "If I'd been brought up totally differently, I might never have needed to look at the adverts in the shop window. Mum would have had a job instead of mooching off the benefit system and spreading her legs to get paid for sex."

Addiction had ruled both of their lives but in completely opposite ways, Mum a slave to the bottle, Janine coping with the fallout from it.

"I'm so feckin' sorry. I didn't know."

"Why would you? I haven't even told the twins it's me. My name was redacted in the newspapers—I was known as Victim C—so when Mason looked into Anna, they wouldn't have seen it. My DCI knows, though. It makes sense why I suspected he was in with The Network, why I didn't trust him. Anna's father..." She sighed again. "A copper. Superintendent. Still, in a weird way I'm glad it happened. I'd never have become a police officer if it hadn't been for the shit that went on inside that house—I wanted to prove that officers weren't all bad, but look how that turned out. I work for the fucking twins. I bet a therapist would have a field day with me."

"What career had ye planned?"

"I'd be a stuffy barrister by now, strutting around court in one of those wigs I imagine smells of dust."

"I can't see ye doin' that. I mean, ye'd have tae wear one of those black cape things."

She laughed. "Hmm, not me, is it?"

"No."

She brought Bastard's face to mind, trying to marry him with the man who'd tormented her. Getting older hadn't been particularly pleasant to him, turning him ugly, or was that because she knew who he really was inside, so even if he was the most handsome man on the planet, she'd still view him as hideous?

Their phones went off at the same time.

"Looks like we've been added to a group chat," she said.

Ichabod got his burner out and read the screen. "Yep. We need tae go tae the warehouse."

Janine smiled. "Good. I've been looking forward to this for years."

Chapter Twenty-Three

Waking from a light sleep—she'd only just dropped off after tossing and turning in the strange bed—Anna stared up at Will, the lamp he'd put on dazzling her eyes. "What's going on? What's happened?" She dreaded his answer. Had Bastard somehow found out where she was? Had he followed them here? Did they need to go somewhere else?

"We need to get Harper looked after," he said.

Her stomach bunched. The thought of handing him over to someone other than George didn't sit well. "What? Why?" She pushed herself up to sitting.

Will stood upright. "They've got the bastard. He's on the way to the warehouse. George said you wanted to be there so…"

"I haven't *got* anyone to watch Harper, though." She glanced over at her son on a nest of blankets on the floor. There wasn't a cot here, so she'd had to make do.

"Debbie's going to do it."

Anna thought about that. She'd seen her in The Angel, Anna's local haunt when she'd first arrived back in London, although she couldn't recall speaking to her. "I don't know her well enough to…"

"You can trust her. She's a good sort. We have to get a move on, because she's with Moon on his estate. It'll take a while to get there, then we'd have to go to the warehouse, which is on Cardigan. That's about an hour all told."

Now faced with the enormity of watching Bastard die, Anna wasn't sure she could do it. "I…"

"I get it, I really do—been through similar to this myself, going to the warehouse and whatever—but if you don't go, you might regret it. If you're stuck here and you change your mind, it might be too late to get you there in time. George won't hang about—unless he's in one of his extra-long torturing moods."

"He said he had medieval tools."

"Ah, then he's going to draw it out. Anyway, come on." Will crouched to swaddle Harper in one of the blankets then picked him up. "I put a bag together for him."

She got out of bed, so tired from the disturbed night she'd already had, and pretty emotional now it had come to this. She'd known the twins would find him, it was what she'd wanted, but…

Stop dithering. Just go.

She put her clothes and shoes on that they'd bought in Tesco, glad she'd had a shower before bed—she'd been sticky from the sweat of fear on the way here. She left the room and found Will in the lounge. Anna checked the bag he'd packed, just to make sure there was everything her son needed and, satisfied he'd thought of everything, she picked it up and followed him out to the car.

In the back seat, she held Harper and strapped them in. Will drove away, and her mind raced with various scenarios. Someone snatching Harper off Debbie. Bastard getting free from his restraints and going for Anna. Him telling her things she didn't want to know.

She glanced at the time on the dash. Half two in the morning. How long would it take to kill him? She had to be at the salon by nine, the staff would turn up by then. Or had George opted to close it? That wouldn't be good for business. The booking ledger was full, so it would mean disappointing people.

"The salon," she said.

"Talk to George about it. He won't expect you to work when you've not had much sleep."

"I know, but I want to open up. I *have* to. I want it to be the best hairdresser's around, and letting people down won't exactly put me a good light, will it."

"Play it by ear."

Twenty minutes later, he pulled up outside a massive house in its own grounds. The light beside the front door came on, and Debbie emerged, her dressing gown cord tied tightly. A man followed, much older than her, and they approached the car.

Debbie opened the back door. "All right?"

"Not really," Anna said. "My son...I've never..."

"He'll be fine. I'll treat him like he's my own, okay? Give him here."

Anna undid the seat belt and kissed Harper's head. Tears stung her gritty eyes.

"Don't be daft," Debbie said. "This isn't the long goodbye. You'll see him in a few hours." She took the baby. "Aww, he's lovely. Moon, get his bag for me, will you, love?"

Debbie stepped back, and Moon took her place, leaning in.

He grabbed the bag and lifted it over Anna. "Your boy will be treated like a prince, so don't go worrying."

His voice, so rough and loud, had Anna shrinking back. "Thank you."

"What's his feeding times?"

"Breakfast about seven, lunch at one if I'm not back by then."

"Does he like pureed fruit? We've been Googling." He smiled widely.

Anna nodded, pleased they'd thought of Harper and his needs. "Banana and strawberries if you have them, but only a quarter of a banana blended in because it'll be too heavy. He has milk in between the solids, seven ounces. The bottles and milk powder are in that bag. You'll need to sterilise and—"

"Yep, right. It's all in hand." He stood and went to Debbie, looking down at Harper. "Is he making you broody?"

"Fuck off," Debbie said. "You're enough of a baby for me, thanks."

"Oi, don't go letting people know that!"

Anna got out to go to the passenger side at the front. As Debbie and Moon took her precious bundle into the house, the tears fell. Would Harper panic when he woke and she wasn't there? She got in the car, swiping the wetness away, hating the lump in her throat. Seat belt clipped in, she stared ahead.

"He'll be okay with them," Will said. "I promise."

She nodded, and he swung the car in an arc so it faced the driveway.

On the road again, Anna imagined what lay ahead. What were those medieval tools? What on earth would George do to Bastard? Would he *really* shove one of them up his arse and twist?

She shuddered at the thought.

"You okay?" Will asked.

"Not really."

"It's a weird one, isn't it, when you finally get the chance to tell people what they did to you, how they made you feel, knowing they can't walk away."

"You said you've been through it. How did you manage, you know, after?"

"Fine. I felt vindicated. Like I never had to worry about anything again. The twins look after me. They're my family now, plus Debbie and Martin. He's the one who collects the protection money. Nice bloke. They saved him, too."

"Sounds like they save a lot of people."

"They do. Listen, why don't you have a kip for half an hour?"

She closed her eyes, but Bastard danced behind her eyelids, as did the other two fuckers. As if in a dream, she walked through the house of her childhood, remembering so many happy times, tainted by what they'd done. As she'd got older, she'd patched it all together, realising the game she'd played with the babysitters wasn't really a game but a trap. The scream, the spider.

How cruel they'd been to use a child in that way. She'd never dream of doing that to Harper.

She drifted off, glad of the oblivion.

Chapter Twenty-Four

*N*ervous, *Valandra now had doubts about what she'd done. Rusty could open her mouth to David or Sidney, tell them what she'd said. She could fuck this whole thing up. Valandra could, of course, deny ever speaking to her during the night, say Rusty had made it up to bring about discord, and they'd believe that because she'd paused the recording for the time it had taken her to speak. David might check, but*

he'd see Rusty had been asleep the whole time—Valandra had already spliced the video after pretending to Rusty that David had woken up. She'd had enough hours in the day to have studied the cameras and how they worked, how to edit. After the murders had been committed, she'd erase every recording that included her and Anna. She'd be safe, free of suspicion. She'd impress upon Anna how important it was for them to say they hadn't known women were downstairs. She may have to resort to threatening her, though...

Even with the footage doctored, it had been a risk whispering to Rusty.

Have I thought this through properly?

Maybe not. Rusty could ruin the whole thing.

Am I willing to get caught in order to save Anna?

How alien, to realise she loved the child more than herself. How freeing. All her life, she'd groused about her lot, angry at her parents for using her as free labour. She'd vowed never to let anyone rule her again—and there she'd gone, plummeting feetfirst into David and Sidney's pool, swallowed up by the water. Gladly drowning in the life they'd given her. Maybe the honeymoon phase was finally over, although it had gone on for much longer than the usual. Years.

If Anna didn't exist, would this even be happening? Would Valandra have lain there the past few nights, concocting a plan to escape? Or would she have still been so enamoured with her husband and his brother? If not for Anna, she may never have woken up.

While she had those sexual penchants and always would, now that Anna's wellbeing was at stake, Valandra couldn't stand by and allow that child to be caged any longer. If she didn't manage to run away with her when Rusty had played her part, then she'd… She didn't know what she'd do.

Had she been rash?

Would Rusty supposedly killing the men be classed as self-defence? The police would question why she'd needed to kill them when they'd been drugged. Would Rusty be so desperate to be set free that she'd agree to the terms—risking going to prison?

God, I really haven't planned this very well.

Maybe talking it through with Rusty would clear up some of the iffy areas.

With Anna asleep, courtesy of a little medicine, and David at work, Valandra went to the fuse box and shut down the electricity—that way, she could pretend to David there had been a power cut, not that she'd purposely needed the cameras off. She collected the carrier bag of shopping he'd bought last night so he'd know she'd done as he'd asked, then went downstairs and opened the flat door to deliver it.

With the electric off and no windows to provide light, an emergency, battery-operated ceiling bulb had come on. Rusty sat on the sofa, and in the murky glow, she eyed Valandra warily. Picked at one of her cuticles. Shook her head as though she thought her ridiculous.

Valandra bristled at that, but she couldn't let Rusty get to her. She had to stay in control. Closing then locking the door, she slipped the key in her trouser pocket and took the bag over to the kitchen area. "The cameras are off. This conversation will be between you and me—and I hope it stays that way. I'm trusting you here."

Rusty scoffed. "Trusting me! Fucking hell, you're something else. You lock me up for weeks, treat me like shit, rape me with your pervert of a husband and his weirdo brother, yet you're trusting me, like I should be grateful? Piss off."

Stunned by the vitriol, the gall of the woman, Valandra tamped down her need to hit her. "I understand you must be feeling animosity towards me, and I don't blame you."

"Kind of you."

Valandra kept her back to Rusty and closed her eyes for a moment. "You could hit me, right this second, take the key, and go. Anna's asleep. No one else is upstairs. I could say you overpowered me and escaped. But that wouldn't solve the issue I want to fix."

"Which is?"

"Anna."

"Right, so all of a sudden you give a shit about what she's going through, do you? Eight years after she was born, you care. That child has been kept inside this house all of her life—no school, no friends, just whacko parents and an uncle for company—and it's only now you've realised it's wrong?"

"Put like that… I was caught up in what I wanted, how I felt. I had a lifetime of being oppressed, much like you, and I wanted something for me. I've been blinded. I should never have agreed to Anna being born." Did that sound plausible? Like she really was sorry?

"Spare me the pity story. Loads of people grow up oppressed, but you don't see them doing what you've done, do you. The amount of cases I've read where offenders blame their childhood, as if that's a good enough excuse for what they've done. It plays a part, yes, but you still have the bit of yourself that knows it's wrong. But I forgot, you're obviously a fucking psychopath—or a sociopath, I haven't worked out which it is yet. All of you are mental in the head, and that poor kid's stuck in the middle."

"Which is what I've realised." Valandra emptied the bag: oranges, bread, deodorant. Chocolates—oh God, chocolates meant… "We have to get out of here, do you understand?"

"We? You're one of the fucking abductors!"

Valandra spun round and faced her. Held her temper in check. She lifted the chocolates and waved them in the air. "Do you understand what this means?"

"What, a box of Milk Tray?"

"They're your last treat."

"This is another one of your games. I'm not falling for it."

"He lied to you. We didn't 'find' Lacey dead in the shower—he slit her wrists. We didn't 'find' Shania dead in bed—he came down while I was asleep and strangled her. You've had two periods, and to him it doesn't look like this is working. He ranted about bringing someone else down here, another woman. The chocolates mean he's decided to bloody kill you. Now will you listen?"

"But I haven't come on again—I could be pregnant."

"You're due on tomorrow, we've kept tabs. If that doesn't happen…" Valandra sighed. Felt this slipping away. Felt out of control. "Look, I don't care what happens to you, I really don't, I just want to get Anna out. I can't do that with him and Sidney alive. David will find us, take her away from me, lock her up again. I still love the man, but I love Anna more. I need you to help me."

"I thought you didn't care what happened to me. If you need me, then you'd better start fucking caring. What's the plan?"

"I'm going to drug them, kill them, but you need to say it was you when the police come—you'll get away with it because you've been held captive. You'll say you've never seen me before, that I had nothing to do with this. It was all David and Sidney."

"Will you listen to yourself? Anna's going to tell them everything; she's not stupid, you know. And you expect me to let you walk away after everything you've done to me? I've got bite marks on my body, ones that will scar—and they match your teeth. You whipped me, you shoved things inside me and laughed. You're off your tree, yet I'm supposed to just let you take that innocent kid and fuck off to treat other people the same way?"

Valandra, used to getting what she wanted since she'd killed her parents, didn't like Rusty denying her needs. Her instinct was to slap the shit out of her, to force her to comply, but she had the sense to know it wouldn't work this time. "Listen, I understand your hatred towards me, but this is about Anna. This is about stopping those men — stopping David from having another child and doing the same thing all over again. I don't want her feeling like I did. I don't want her turning out like me!"

Rusty stared at her, assessing. "This could be a trick. I said that last night when you whispered to me. Forgive me if I don't trust you." She rolled her eyes.

"Fine. I'll do it myself tonight. Drug them with Anna's medicine, slit their throats, and take Anna. I'll go on the run, whatever, but I'm not letting her stay here any longer."

"You're serious."

Valandra nodded. "God help me, but for the first time in my life, I care about someone more than myself."

"I don't think you should take Anna. You're...not well in the head. How can I let you walk off with her, knowing what you're capable of? And if you go on the run, it means keeping her hidden, so you'll be taking her away to a life the same as this one — no friends, no school, nothing. You haven't thought this through properly."

Valandra bit her lip. She hadn't *thought that far. She'd assumed Rusty would be so desperate to get out that she'd agree to anything. "Fuck."*

Rusty smiled, then chuckled. "D'you know what? If you love Anna as much as you seem to think, then you'll give her up, let her go to her mother's family. You'll admit what you did to me and let them put you away. You need to serve time for this shit."

The thought of that soured Valandra's stomach. Her, in a cell? Other women around her, unwashed and smelly? No. Absolutely not. "I'll change. I'll never do anything like this again."

Rusty laughed, the sound full of derision. "You enjoyed *what you did. It's a part of you. I can't see you changing. Anna gets taken to her family or nothing. I won't say I killed those two perverts unless you agree to that."*

Valandra nodded, although she wouldn't hold up her end of the bargain.

Rusty still had a lot to learn about the workings of a criminal mind.

Alone again, Rusty blinked at the lights coming back on. Valandra had laid out her plan from start to

finish. It would happen tonight—Sidney was coming to dinner, and she'd dose their wine with the medicine. That was all very well, but the strength of the liquid might not be high because it had been prescribed for a child, so she'd have to use a lot of it. What if it didn't work? What if they tasted it? She'd asked Valandra that, but she'd waved the concern away.

So many things had still been left up in the air. How would Rusty explain the fact she'd supposedly found the medicine, knew what it was used for, and decided to put it in the men's drinks? How, even though she'd be able to leave the flat because the door would be unlocked, was she supposed to believably creep upstairs, root around for said medicine, and even get it into their glasses without them seeing her in an open-plan area? Why would she need to kill them if they'd fallen asleep? The police wouldn't buy that as a coincidence, and she might be charged for murder because she hadn't needed to kill them.

Okay, Valandra planned to unlock the doors when the men had fallen asleep, so Rusty could come upstairs and find them sprawled out on the sofa and supposedly kill them, but really? Valandra was the one who'd wield the knife, and she'd get blood on her. She'd need a shower—and the police would scour the house and know blood had gone down the drain. Rusty wouldn't have the correct blood spatter patterns on her to fake the fact she was the killer. It would be obvious the scene had been staged. As for Valandra erasing the camera recordings... Didn't she know it could be retrieved from the hard drive?

Not that Rusty cared about that, because she wasn't playing the game the way Valandra wanted her to. She didn't believe that woman would allow Anna to go to her mother's family. She was going to go on the run, like she'd said earlier.

She said she'd take Anna to the cinema for the evening, returning to the carnage, her husband and brother-in-law dead, her screaming, poor Anna witnessing it all. She'd find the police here, as Rusty was supposed to run to a neighbour after she'd slashed their throats and tell them she'd been held captive. No, it wasn't going to happen that way. Never.

But Rusty had agreed to the plan while making one of her own.

Valandra had a lot to learn about someone who'd studied the criminal mind.

Chapter Twenty-Five

Greg would never admit it, but he was a bit breathless. He hadn't helped George wrestle Bastard into the warehouse, that would have been too much, and he watched the proceedings, asking himself if he'd ever be the same again. Ichabod had gone back to Jackpot Palace to check everything had been okay in his absence, and Janine had gone into the bathroom with

Cameron. George set up his latest medieval contraption, the upright ring that Bastard would crouch in. For once, Greg felt the upcoming torture matched the crime. No amount of pain was good enough in this instance.

Being shot hadn't done a number on him like it had with George. Greg hadn't had much time to think about it at the time beyond the burning in his chest, him hitting the floor, and Moon dragging him away. Oh, and the wrench inside him just before he'd closed his eyes on that steel table. George had said at the point Greg had died, *he'd* felt that wrench, too. Greg had always known twins had a strange, unexplainable bond, but that night had proved it beyond doubt.

Bastard had been roped to the wooden chair in the usual fashion, naked, his dick shrivelling. Now Greg understood what it was like to die, to be pulled away so softly, so gently, these sessions would hold a new meaning for him. There hadn't been a tunnel with a white light at the end, just darkness, but it was the nice kind, pillowy and serene. He'd never tell George that; his brother wanted their victims to suffer when taking their final breath, and to be told they likely hadn't and wouldn't suffer in the future, he'd get a cob on.

Even though the body hurt, in Greg's experience, his mind went somewhere else in the last few seconds, shielding him from the agony. Mum's voice, beautiful in that dark void, had infused him with the need to go to her, to float towards it.

"No, son. Piss off back to your brother, he can't be left on his own," she said. *"You're not meant to be here yet."*

The mention of his twin had sent him back to that room in the abattoir, the light above blinding, George's sobs and screams filling his ears, and for a brief moment, Greg had wanted to go back into the blackness as a wash of pain had overtaken him.

"He's breathing." Lincoln.

"Oh, thank fuck." George.

"Quick, we'll get him to the clinic." Moon.

Greg had passed out again, waking after his operation.

He blinked back the tears and stuffed the emotions down. He'd yet to tell George about Mum—Greg reckoned it was just an auditory hallucination, his brain firing wrong at the time of passing over, or he'd just *wished* she'd spoken so it wouldn't feel so upsetting to die. George would insist it *was* her, though. He'd grab on to any chance that she was still out there somewhere, watching over them. That way, he didn't have to let her go.

In the two weeks he'd been recuperating, Greg had had a lot of time to think. To assess whether the estate and his way of life was what he *really* wanted. The fact that he didn't know how to do anything else was a stumbling block in walking away—they could, of course, go back to being hired menaces, maybe for Moon, but that was still dangerous. But his need to be by George's side, to make the East End the best part of London, overruled any of his musings about moving into the country to their dream cottage, the one they'd imagined as kids when Richard had ruled the roost.

He stared at Bastard and imagined how he was feeling. He hadn't appeared to twig yet that the Grim Reaper waited in the wings. Who would call out to *him* in the black void? Did he have someone he loved, and who loved him, waiting to pull him wherever you went when you snuffed it?

Bastard eyed him, then George, the 'they're twins' realisation clearly slapping him in the face.

Greg stepped closer. "The shit you did to those women... Who the fuck do you think you are?"

Bastard blanched then sighed as though Greg exasperated him. "Another one who doesn't understand. That copper didn't either. She said I'm a pervert."

"You are." Greg shoved his hands in his pockets to stop himself from walloping him one. His chest wouldn't thank him for the exertion. "You should never have been let out. You've already proved you're still a danger to society by wanting to snatch Anna."

"I don't want to snatch her, I want to take her with me."

"Same thing."

"Do *you* know where she is? Where that man took her?"

"Yes, I know where she is. She'll be here soon, as a matter of fact."

"Oh, thank God." Bastard closed his eyes. "Thank *you*."

Greg frowned. *He's a banana short of a bunch.* "We didn't arrange for her to come so you can fuck off with her, you pissflap."

Bastard opened his eyes. "What?"

Greg smiled. "She's going to watch my brother kill you."

Janine paced the bathroom in the warehouse, nervous about revealing herself to Bastard. She'd got into her car at the air-raid house and driven here behind Ichabod so her tormenter hadn't seen her. She'd entered the warehouse directly behind George and Bastard, dipping into the bathroom while his back had been turned. She wasn't ready to confront him yet.

For years she'd imagined this moment, her full of confidence like she'd learned to be, striding out to face him, but now it had come to it, a nugget of her old insecurities had crept in. He'd reduced her to a crying, wailing mess. He'd seen her naked. He'd laughed at her tears. No matter that she'd grown into a strong, independent woman, those things would stay with her forever.

"What's bothering you?" Cameron asked from his perch on the closed toilet seat. "Is it that you're a copper yet you're going to watch them kill someone? I thought you'd done that before so it wouldn't bother you."

"I have, and it doesn't, but this bloke's different." Considering her growing feelings for Cameron, she owed it to him to explain everything now, not subject him to the shock at the same time as Bastard. She already felt bad that Ichabod knew before anyone else, but he'd caught her in an unguarded moment, and in the darkness of the garden, no one to see the tears pouring down her face, she'd taken the chance to unburden herself.

"*Why* is he different?"

She took a deep breath. "You know I told you about the women, Lacey, Shania, and Rusty?" She faced the door so he couldn't read her expression. See the anguish on her face. With him, she'd always been brash and in control. Him seeing her teetering on the edge of an abyss wasn't something she wanted to put him through.

"Yeah…"

Another deep breath. "I'm Rusty."

"Jesus Christ, Janine…"

He came up behind her, wrapping his arms around her waist, holding her tight, making her feel as if she was safe and no one could ever hurt her again. She leaned back, liking the comfort a bit too much, needing it, and placed her hands over his overlapping ones on her stomach. If they could just stay like this, no words, she could get her emotions back on track.

"That's why you're reluctant to have a relationship."

She wanted to ignore him but couldn't leave it there. It was time to open up, but she worried that by doing so she'd break the dam. "Hmm. Men are arseholes, present company excluded. What they did to me…it's scarred deep. I know normal sex and what I went through with them are two completely different things, I've tried it with a couple of one-night stands and one bloke I was with for a short while, but my brain…I inevitably think of *that*, what it was like, and I clam up. In the end, I just didn't bother. Didn't see the bloody point."

"Have you been to a therapist?"

"No, but it was offered at the time. I should have. I *could* have years later, but I didn't like Janet, and Vic's…"

"…a man."

"Yes." *He gets it. Understands.* "So even though we've kissed, you and me, I haven't been able to…go further. I want to, I just…I need you to know it isn't you, it's me."

"You don't have to do anything until you're ready. I'll wait. For however long it takes. You've got under my skin."

Tears stung, and she hated them. *Hated them.* They were for weak people, and she didn't want to be weak.

They're not. They show you're human.

So *tired* of fighting this battle alone, for being a one-woman mountain, unshakeable in the face of adversity, she turned in his arms but couldn't look at him. He rested a finger beneath her chin and tipped it up. She stared at his face, avoiding his eyes.

"I'm broken," she said, "You need to know that."

He kissed her forehead. "Then I'll fix you."

Chapter Twenty-Six

George, in his forensic suit, had finished setting up his crushing device and now slapped the Pear of Anguish against his palm. He'd only used it once before and looked forward to doing so again. It had petal-like claws on the end that, when closed, resembled a flower bud, but if he turned the screw at the top, the petals opened out on the other end as far as a daisy's. Painful.

He'd told Anna he'd shove it up this prick's arse, and he'd make sure that happened.

"See this?" He did a demonstration for his captive's benefit.

Bastard stared, wide-eyed.

"Imagine that up your jacksie." George laughed. "Worse than a case of piles, eh?" He strutted back and forth in front of him—what the fuck was holding Janine up? "Did you enjoy your little chat with our copper?"

"No, she's…she's not a nice person."

"And *you* are? Sodding hell. I'm not even going to bother asking you why you did the shit you did because, quite frankly, I don't want to hear it all over again just yet. It's sickening. You can explain yourself to Anna when she gets here, though. I'm sure she'd like to hear your take on why an innocent little girl was hidden away, not to mention three women held against their will."

"It was because…because of the abduction."

"Right, well, I don't know what you're on about, but like I said, you can tell Anna." George checked his phone. Will should be here soon, so in the meantime, he'd have a bit of fun. He walked to the tool table and put the device down, selecting a battery-operated blowtorch. He returned to stand in front of Bastard. "I noticed your fingers need cauterising. A nasty mess you've got there."

Bastard flinched. "Please, no, just leave my fingers alone."

"You haven't fucking *got* any on that hand! By the way, there's no anaesthetic here, so you might want to grit your teeth, sunshine."

George crouched and inspected the fingers, or what was left of them. Personally, he'd have lopped off the thumb an' all. The remains, swollen from the snipping, plus bloated from the pressure of the rope coiled around his middle, pinning his arms to his sides, appeared grotesque. He switched the torch on and held the blue heat to the stubs. The man screamed, flapping his hand, and George followed its movement with the torch. Bored, he switched off the flame and put the torch back on the table. Bastard whimpered, asking God to stop this, but the big bloke in the clouds wasn't listening, just like he hadn't for Anna, Lacey, Shania, and Rusty.

George went back with his cricket stump; it deserved a little outing. He put the pointed end into one of Bastard's ears. Pushed it farther in. This scream, louder than the last, had George smiling.

At the table, he switched the stump for a medieval tool.

"Fuck me," Greg said.

George laughed. "You watch. It'll be fun."

"Not for him, it won't."

"That's the point. This only arrived the other day, and I've been dying to try it out." George stood in front of Bastard. "Look at this beauty."

He held it up. Two rectangular wooden blocks, thick black screws near the edges, halfway down. On the inner parts of the blocks, rows and rows of long, conical metal spikes.

"You're...you're mentally ill," Bastard said.

"Takes one to know one." George cocked his head. "Aww, did you think I'd be offended by you saying that? Fuck off. I *know* I'm not right in the head dot com, unlike you, Mr Denial."

He slid Bastard's leg between the blocks and turned the mouse-ear handles of the black screws to draw the boards together until the spike tips kissed his skin.

"When I keep going, those spikes are going to dig in, meet in the middle. This is called a Knee

Splitter, but as you can see, I'm just going for the lower leg. Giss a hand, bruv."

Greg crouched and gripped one screw handle. George took command of the other.

George grinned at a shaking Bastard. "Hold your breath, my old son, here comes the sting!"

Together, they twisted. The boards compressed, the spikes bit into the flesh, and they kept going, the metal teeth disappearing into the leg altogether to the symphony of the tosser's screams. George winked at his brother, chuffed to bits they were a pair at work again, and Greg shook his head, likely knowing George enjoyed this.

"Enough," Greg said. "We don't want him passing out."

"Too late."

Bastard's head dropped back, his eyes closed.

They undid the screws. Taking the leg out, George put the device on the floor and inspected the wounds amidst the streams of blood. Bits of muscles and flesh peeked out from each hole, claret pooling on the floor.

"Messy cunt," he muttered and rose, holding out a hand for Greg, instinctively knowing he needed it to help him stand.

Greg wiped sweat of his forehead. "Think I'll stick the PlayStation on."

George frowned. "You all right?"

"Yep, just need a breather."

"Too much too soon. I *knew* you shouldn't have come back to work yet."

"Shut your fucking smug cakehole." Greg wandered off and slumped onto the sofa.

George, angry his twin might be hurting, followed and sat next to him. "There's no shame in admitting this is too much for you."

"I know. Like I said, I just need a breather. I've been in bed for two sodding weeks, so this feels like I've run a marathon."

"So long as you're okay."

George got up, and his phone bleeped. He checked the message.

Bastard woke up and screamed again.

"Shut up!" George barked.

The man snapped his mouth closed, whimpering, viscous green snot dangling over his lips.

"Calm your tits now. Anna's here."

George went to let them in but stepped outside first to have a chat. Will already had a key to the gate in their car park, and he closed the padlock then walked over, Anna coming with him.

"Right, I've already started, so he's in a bit of a shit state." George smiled. Shrugged. "I got bored waiting."

"Has he…has he said why he wants to see me?" Anna asked.

"Sounds to me like he planned on kidnapping you and Harper, wants to 'keep you hidden'. Said he needs to smother your son—and I've only told you that so you don't go feeling sorry for him. He's fucked up in the head, Ichabod and Janine have confirmed that, but whatever, I don't care. He needs to pay for what he's done."

"So he went loopy in the nick?" Will asked.

"Unless he's been that way all along and has been hiding it."

"Makes sense," Anna muttered. "They all seemed like good people to outsiders, even to me, so they know how to be two different people. When I was old enough to know, Nan and Grandad Barker started telling me a bit about what happened to the women, but I shut them down. I didn't Google the case, didn't want to know, but now maybe I should so it gives me the impetus to hurt him."

"It involves a lot of rape and torture," George said, "so you're better off not knowing the ins and outs."

"I had a feeling."

"Are you ready to go in?"

Anna nodded.

Janine walked out of the bathroom and stopped short. She'd known Anna was coming, but she didn't expect her to look exactly the same as the child she'd known, just an older version. Her chest squeezed tight, her breathing caught, and it took a moment for normal function to resume.

Anna glanced her way, and her hand flew up to her mouth. "Rusty?"

So she recognised me even with my hair dyed.

Tears blurred Janine's vision, and she couldn't speak, her mind going back to little Anna in the flat, David racing down there to save her from the spider. "Run," she'd mouthed, and Janine had known then that she should have trusted her instinct the first time she'd knocked on the front door of that hideous house, walked away, never looked back. She blinked, the tears falling, and swiped them away.

"Rusty?" George said. "What the fuck?"

"Leave it," Cameron said.

Anna swallowed. "Oh God, I'm *so sorry* for what they did to you."

"Not your fault," Janine muttered, sounding brisker than she'd intended. "We'll talk later, but for now we need to sort *him* out."

Anna's gaze wrenched from Janine and landed on Bastard. She pelted forward, launching herself at him, and slapped, scratched, and punched him over and over, animalistic noises coming out of her. Janine watched on, knowing that feeling well, the need to hurt him, to give him pain. She wished she'd given in and done the same at the air-raid shelter, venting all her frustration on him instead of calmly snipping off his fingers. But she'd taught herself to be controlled, to keep her emotions in check, never letting anyone know how she really felt. She'd allowed the demented trio to see her vulnerability, her agony, and hear her pleading for them to stop, and since then, no one else had been allowed that privilege.

Until Cameron. The dam had burst at last, and she'd cried into his chest after he'd said he'd fix her, great racking sobs that had scored her throat. He'd stroked her hair and remained silent, giving her time to let it out, although she'd cut it short, because unleashing the lot all at once would mean she'd have no energy for this part now.

Anna stumbled back, slipping on the blood that had puddled on the floor from Bastard's leg. She breathed heavily, her hair partly covering her face, eyes wet and flashing.

"Anna," he croaked. "Anna…"

"You don't deserve to say my name," she spat. "You don't deserve *anything* except what's coming your way."

She presented her back to him, and he swept his gaze to Janine. A creepy, leering smile transformed his ugly mouth, and she was back there, in the flat, him sitting in the corner and watching, egging David and Valandra on.

"Hello, arsehole," she said. "I wonder how it's going to feel now the tables have turned. Let's see, shall we?" She looked at George and answered his silent question. "Later, all right?"

He frowned. "Why didn't you ever say?"

"*Later*." She gritted her teeth and took a deep breath. "Now, where's that pear you told me about?"

Chapter Twenty-Seven

The smugness he'd experienced when Rusty had come out of that doorway rapidly evaporated at the mention of the pear. She was going to inflict on him what they'd inflicted on her. The ultimate revenge. He kept the fear off his face, though, still leering at her, wanting her to feel every degrading thought that paraded through his head. She stared at him, didn't so much as flinch, but her red-rimmed eyes and blotchy face reminded him of how she'd looked in the flat when they'd abused her. She'd been crying so wasn't as tough as she thought. *Now* he understood why she'd stayed in the darkness in that weird underground bunker. She hadn't wanted him to see her. So what was different for her to have revealed herself now?

They said he was mad, and he was—but only mad that life hadn't turned out the way he'd envisaged. He'd admit that what he'd said to them had likely brought them to the conclusion that he had mental health issues, but he didn't. Why should he explain himself so they understood what he was getting at? All he wanted was to keep Anna and Harper safe, it was all he could think about and all they needed to know.

A great whoosh of cold sluiced through him, taking him unawares. Seeing Rusty again had brought back the old thoughts. Was there another family member out there? Had she been pregnant? There hadn't been a trial because they'd confessed, pleaded guilty, so he hadn't seen her again until now. Her name hadn't been used in any of the newspapers, so Warson hadn't found her. David had never mentioned her real name after he'd done a search on her, preferring to stick to her nickname so it was less personal — they'd learned from the other two not to let emotions become involved — but it was the other way around, wasn't it? A nickname was more intimate. David had said if they called her Rusty, they could pretend she wasn't Janine, convince themselves that, if her disappearance was reported, it wasn't her.

One of the twins went behind him to the table and reappeared with that horrible contraption. "Give me a hand, Will."

Where's a paracetamol when you need one? His leg hurt so much it had gone numb, the pain in his ear worse as his eardrum had perforated. He dare not look at his fingers.

Anna spun round.

"Please, Anna," he said. "It's not safe for you and your son to be out there."

"Fuck off," she muttered and gave him a scathing look.

"Oh, for fuck's sake," Rusty said to him. "Stop banging on about that."

It hurt, Anna's stare, his heart panging for what could have been if she'd been shielded forever. He'd lost so many years of her growing up, didn't know her anymore, but it was clear from the language she'd just used that she'd been exposed to the rough element, exactly what they hadn't wanted.

"Did you have a baby?" he asked Rusty, eyeing her up and down to put her back in her place. To set off her memories like she'd done to him earlier in the bunker. Bitch.

"No, I had a coil fitted."

He narrowed his eyes at her.

She laughed at him. "You didn't know that, did you? My little weapon against you all. Shame 'our man' didn't dig a little deeper to discover that."

It was a blessing she hadn't conceived. He'd have hated for that poor child to be brought up by the likes of her. She'd turned into a cruel woman.

Will and the twin approached.

"Want me to untie him, George?"

"Yeah."

Will undid the ropes, and the release of pressure from his raging-hot hand, which still burned from the blowtorch, was instant. Will yanked him to his feet, and his bad leg wouldn't hold him up. Those spikes had gone into the muscles.

"Put him facedown on the floor and sit on his back," George ordered. "Trap his arms with your knees."

Will took his legs out from under him and let him fall forward. He smacked onto the concrete, banging his nose, blood gushing, pain blooming into his head. He turned his face to the side so he could look at Anna, make sure she was okay.

Will sat on him, pushing the breath from his lungs.

"Spread his legs," Rusty said. "And give me that pear."

Someone gripped his ankles and wrenched his legs apart. He couldn't see that far round, but he sensed Rusty kneeling in the gap. He stared over at the head of the other twin who sat on the sofa. A TV, on silent, showed some kind of game with guns. He focused on that and tried to zone out.

Something prodded at his backside, preventing him from taking himself away inside his head. His arsehole instinctually clenched to stop the attempted intrusion, and Rusty applied more force.

"Want a hammer to hit the end with?" George asked.

"No."

Rusty shoved at the pear so hard it shot inside, then came the feeling of his rectum splitting, and blood, hot and wet, and pain, so much pain. A fumbling sensation, him getting fuller and fuller, his hole stretching, ripping, the petals expanding. He laughed despite the agony, recalling the women, and oh, how those girls had screamed.

"I feel what you did," he shouted. "You hear that, Rusty? We're the same now." His cock hardened at the memories of witnessing her torment, hearing her cries.

"You're *nothing* like me." She pushed one final time.

He screamed, his eyes bulging.

Anna strode towards him and kicked him in the face. More pain, his already broken nose skewing, and through the stream of his eyes watering, he smiled at her, blood coating his teeth, spreading on his tongue, going down the back of his throat, choking him. His whole body was on fire, his mind going lucid, and he floated above it all.

Then nothing.

The next time he came round, he couldn't breathe properly. He squatted, his chest clamped to his thighs, his chin on his knees, lower arms around his shins. Unnerved by being moved and manipulated without his knowledge, he shivered. Something pressed on the top of his bowed back, his upper arms. A tightness encompassed him, and he looked to the left, then the right. Something metal—a large upright ring?—surrounded him. Anna and Rusty stood either side.

"All right, my old son?" George asked from somewhere.

The pressure increased, the metal closing tighter.

"Anna's been turning the screw at the top to make the ring smaller," George said casually. "In the end, if she wants it to go that far, it's going to crush your bones and flatten your lungs. You'll suffocate to death."

Staring at the floor to steady the panic, he didn't have enough air inside him to say anything.

I thought I was supposed to tell Anna why I needed to take her away? Why are they killing me instead?

"Please," he managed to push out, but it was an extreme effort, and he tried to suck oxygen back in. His lungs were too flattened to expand, and he panted, experiencing that horrible sensation when swimming underwater, where the surface was too far away and you thought you'd drown before you reached it.

"Your go, Janine," George said.

The ring squeezed again. It emphasised the pain in his lower leg, and liquid heat dripped down his skin—the contraption forced blood out of all the holes from the spikes. Something inside him cracked—his spine?—and an almighty burst of agony shot up it. With not enough lung capacity to scream, he sipped air rather than attempt to take in a big breath, panting, his mouth open, his chest burning. His head lightened, blackness descending, white spots dancing.

"I've changed my mind now. Not about him telling me things, I still don't want to know. But I want him chopped up," Anna said.

What?

An incremental release, the ring expanding maybe an inch. Then more and more until he imagined himself as the petals of that pear, unfurling. Blessed air entered his lungs, and with every turn of the screw to release him, more pain came in staggered degrees, each muscle, tendon, and bone filling with it. Dragged by his hair backwards, he left the ring, was dumped on the floor, every part of him suffering. Even his gums ached.

"You deserved that," Rusty said and stood over him holding an electric saw. "And this."

She bent, pressed a button, and the circular blade whizzed to life. He stared at it in horror, and she brought it closer, the cool displacement of air brushing his skin. She lowered it, and it bit through his upper arm. Pain like no other streaked through it, hot and livid, and he turned his face away, blood splashing onto his chest and neck, his cheek.

Something—or some*one*—fumbled with his penis, cold steel encasing it around the base. The juxtaposition between the heat in his arm and the arctic freeze of whatever was on his dick merged together, creating a panic attack he didn't want to have. It would show them he was scared, and he didn't want to give them the pleasure. He couldn't suppress it, though, it had a mind of its own, and he hyperventilated.

The saw blade gouged deeper. He screamed, the agony too intense—his arm, his wrecked shin, the stubs on his hand, his ear, his spine—and he welcomed death, something he'd never expected. Savageness ripped at his private parts.

"Do you like my Chappy Chopper?" George shouted. "Does it hurt?"

The moment his penis fell away from his body was the last thing he recalled.

He woke to the sound of general chatter, as though this place was a pub, people getting together for a natter. The absurdity of that, the *normalcy* of it, enraged him. If he had the energy to shout at them, he would, but his body was too broken, his mind muddled by a resurgence of pain, although it didn't hurt as much as it should. Had his mind blocked it out?

He hung from that hideous rack thing on the wall, spikes digging into one side of his back and arse, one wrist bound above to the left, his legs spread, ankles attached to manacles. With no right arm, his torso leaned forward on that side, putting pressure on his secured wrist. Over at the table, the tools had been cleared away. Takeaway bags littered it, coffee and drinks cups in front of each person. The smell of burgers wafted to him, and fries, a hint of bacon.

While he'd been out for the count, they'd all stopped for *food*? They had to be sick in the head if they could torture someone then go about afterwards as if what they'd done didn't matter.

The irony.

He acknowledged it. These people weren't that much different to him if they could switch from torture to the everyday, yet they'd let him know they thought what he'd done was *bad*, living the two sides of his life as he had.

Why were they allowed and he wasn't?

"Ah, he's awake," George said. "Feeling a bit better, are you? I gave you a pain relief injection and cauterised that arm stump with my trusty blowtorch. You're welcome. Mind you, that relief won't last for much longer. I mean, we wouldn't want you not feeling it when Janine chops you up, would we. She asked to take over, see, and who am I to deny her revenge?"

Eyes closed, he blocked out their smiling faces.

Mad, the lot of them.

Chapter Twenty-Eight

*D*avid, *annoyed that the power had gone off today, had lost a chunk of the footage. He liked to watch the day's feed on fast forward while drinking wine after a hard day at work, and it irked him beyond measure that he wasn't able to see what Rusty had been doing for those two hours.*

In the observation room, he watched her on the before-and-after power cut sections to gauge whether she'd done something to trip the electricity, but she'd been sitting on the sofa both times. It must have been as Valandra had said—the people down the road having their driveway dug up had created a problem.

He put the footage on normal speed in real time and smiled. Rusty ate a chocolate. Would that be her last treat? The footage didn't extend to the bathroom, something he'd remedy for the future, so he had no idea whether she'd used a tampon or not, although he supposed he could ask her. His heart leapt—could she be pregnant? Would the next woman he'd selected continue to live her life of freedom after all?

Valandra appeared in the doorway with a wine carafe. He jumped, hadn't heard her climbing the stairs, annoyed at himself for not being alert. She poured him a glass of wine when he'd come in from work, and it had gone to his head more than usual.

"Sidney's had one more than you, so you need to catch up." She topped him up. "Dinner's about to be served."

She left him, and he closed down the computer. The screens turned black, and he picked up his glass and walked downstairs. His vision blurred a little—he really ought to go private and get those early cataracts sorted—and he blinked to clear it. In the lounge area, Sidney sat on the sofa, his head tipped back, eyes closed. David eyed the wine glass his brother held loosely—red wine that would stain the cream fabric if he wasn't careful.

"Watch what you're doing, man." David tutted. "Hold the glass tighter."

Sidney lifted his head. "Sorry, it's been a long day. Bloody exhausted."

"Yes, well…"

David walked to the dining table, one of his shoes catching on the corner of the rug beneath it. He stumbled forward, glass held aloft so he didn't spill any wine. "Fucking thing!" He sat, placing his glass on a coaster. Smiled at Anna who sat opposite. "How was your day, cherub?"

She shrugged. "We did lessons, but I fell asleep after lunch."

David frowned, concern for his daughter dancing inside him. "Are you coming down with something?" He turned towards the living room area. "Sid, come and check her."

Sidney rose and walked over, weaving a bit. "Blimey, I'm more tired than I thought. Let's have a look at you." He put his wine down and felt Anna's forehead then peered at the back of her throat. "No, nothing. You must have just been sleepy."

Valandra came over and handed out serving ladles. "I had a nap, too, so maybe there's something in the air. There wasn't much I could do with the electric going off." She sat and smiled. Took a lid off a tureen and spooned rice onto her plate.

David nosed in the next tureen along—chilli, his favourite. "Ah, you know the way to my heart, darling."

Valandra blushed. "Anything for you." She turned to Sidney. "There's curry in the other one. I know you prefer that."

"Superb." Sidney smiled at Anna. "You want the same as me, don't you."

Anna nodded, and David marvelled at how alike they were, his brother and daughter. Same food tastes, same colouring, same reading preferences. If he was a suspicious man, he'd wonder if Sidney was her father.

He gazed around at his family, which would soon expand if Rusty came through, and an immense surge of pride filled his chest. He'd created this. Anna was being brought up as a child should—protected. He and Valandra were parents who'd never allow her to go outside alone and be abducted, like his parents had done.

The thought of his little sister, the beautiful Anna… He'd named his daughter after her so the original

Anna got to live the life she'd never had. Sidney was of the same mind. This Anna was the other Anna in all respects. They had their sister back, and they'd cherish her, give her everything their sibling had missed out on.

Dinner progressed, David and Sidney encouraged by Valandra to finish the carafe of wine. She'd declined to join them on that indulgence as she wanted to catch up on the two missed hours of schooling from earlier. What a diligent, perfect wife, who treated Anna as her own. How had David got so lucky?

He smiled, content, his eyes drooping.

So lucky.

But his tongue tasted a little odd. That wine had a touch of vinegar about it. Valandra must have bought a new brand. He opened his mouth to ask her, but the words never made it past his lips.

Miraculously, they fell asleep at the same time, their heads slumping forward, chins to chests. Valandra had put two whole bottles of medicine into the carafe. Although it didn't have a taste as such, Anna had said it was bitter, so she always scrunched her nose up when swallowing it.

"Oh my goodness! Daddy and Uncle Sid must be tired." She laughed. "Lazy daisies."

"May I leave the table?" Anna asked.

"Of course. And I've changed my mind about lessons this evening. We're going to the cinema."

Anna's eyes lit up. "Really?"

"Yes. Go upstairs and put on some nice clothes. I'll call you when I'm ready to go."

Anna scampered off, and Valandra waited for the sound of her footsteps on the floor above, then got going. She went into the observation room and sorted the footage. Emptied the recycle bin. Downstairs in the bathroom, she found a hair-dye box in the vanity unit cupboard. She opened it, taking out the gloves and plastic cape. She closed the box and went out into the hallway, popping it in her handbag. In the kitchen, she took her plastic cooking apron off the hook behind the larder door and put it on. Cape and gloves on, too, she returned to the table. Stared at the men she'd loved— still loved—and contemplated taking Anna now, just leaving them here, phoning the police when she was a few miles away, informing them they'd had a woman held in the basement, that she'd drugged them so she could escape, terrified for her life upon finding the captive, who she'd set free.

No, they had to die.

She reached for the serrated knife they'd used to cut the garlic bread at dinner. Decided it might create more mess if she used that. She placed it down and took a smooth-bladed carver from the block on the worktop. Walked around and stood behind David. Gripped his head with one hand, the blade positioned at his neck with the other. Tears burned and fell. She was going to kill the man she was in love with—she'd never find anyone she'd adore as much. Could she do it?

Anna… Think of the child…

She sliced. Stepped back. She looked down at herself—only a couple of speckles of blood on the cape. Then she stared across at Sidney who sat beside a man whose neck gushed blood. The castoff had spattered him, like Rusty had said it would. Valandra stood behind the second man she loved, closed her eyes, and ended him quickly. Forced herself to view her new world through tunnel vision so she didn't see what she'd done—that one glance at David had been enough to hammer home that she'd crossed the line and there was no going back.

She put the knife on the table between the empty chilli and curry dishes and took off the cape and apron, folding it all together and putting it on a chair. She removed the gloves, inside out, and laid them on the apron, then rolled the lot into a sausage, using the apron strings to tie it up. How absurd to think of it as a scroll from years gone by. She shook her head to stop her mind from wandering and placed the scroll in a carrier bag she'd opened and left in the cupboard under the sink, ready. Handles tied, she took it to her handbag and put it inside. She'd dump that and the dye box on the way to the cinema.

So she didn't fully allow herself to acknowledge she'd murdered people—there would be time for tears later when she came home to discover the police here— she unlocked the door to the flat stairway and crept down, although why she crept she had no idea. Anna wouldn't come out of her bedroom until she was called.

At the flat door, she took a deep breath. This part was crucial. Rusty had to wait until Valandra had taken Anna out of the house, making sure the child didn't see her father and uncle dead at the table. Then Rusty would go upstairs, grab the knife, and do whatever she had to in order for blood spatter to land on her skin, her clothes. She wouldn't phone the police until later, wasting the requisite time for her to have found the medicine and drugged the wine. Valandra had said an hour would do. Rusty had queried that— the pathologist would know what time the men had died, or at least they'd have a rough idea. Valandra had wafted her hand to shut her up—the woman thought *she knew it all, just because she read textbooks about criminals. God!*

Valandra unlocked the door. She didn't open it—Rusty would have heard the key turning—and rushed back upstairs, calling, "Anna! Time to go!"

That lovely little girl appeared at the top of the stairs.

"Come down," Valandra said, "but when you get to the bottom, you must close your eyes. I have a surprise for you in the car."

She'd bought another Barbie last week, but David had stopped her from giving it to her, saying it could wait until Anna's birthday next month. Glad of his interference now, Valandra smiled.

Anna came down, and, guiding her to the front door, looping her handbag strap over her shoulder, Valandra reached for the Yale. She took Anna outside, about to close the door, when the prick of something dug into the back of her neck.

"You're not going anywhere."

Rusty.

"Go and wait behind the car, Anna," Rusty said. "I just need to talk to Mummy a minute." Then to

Valandra, quietly, "Nice and slow now. Walk backwards into the house." She dug the knife in harder, splitting the skin and drawing blood.

"You fucking bitch!" Valandra made to run.

Rusty grabbed the woman's perfect bun and yanked her into the house, hating the look Anna cast her way—fear, confusion.

"Mummy…?"

Detesting herself for it, Rusty shut the door and hauled Valandra by the hair to the stairs that led to the flat. The dippy cow had left the key in the lock, and Rusty had thanked her lucky stars. She pushed Valandra down the flight, chasing after her tumbling form, reaching her just as Valandra got to her knees.

"You tricked me, you fucking slag!" she screeched.

Rusty kneed her in the face. Valandra keeled over to the side, screaming, her hands covering her nose, blood seeping through her fingers. Snatching the bun again, Rusty dragged her down the next three stairs then into the flat. She'd like to stand there and tell her exactly what she thought of her, but she didn't have the time. Anna would likely be crying on the driveway, worried, afraid, and she was the most important thing now. Rusty dashed out, locked the door, and put the key in her pocket. Racing upstairs, she headed for the front door, slinging it open and flying out to Anna.

"I want my mummy," Anna mumbled, knuckling her eyes.

But she's not your real mummy…

"It's okay, she's had to stay inside. Let's go and see one of the neighbours so we can use their phone, all right?"

Rusty took her hand and led her across the road to the house directly opposite. She knocked on the door, adrenaline high but a sense of justice having been served warming her tummy. An elderly man answered, his shirt crisp, the knot of his tie perfect, and she imagined he lived an idyllic life where the likes of David, Valandra, and Sidney were a world away from him. What they'd done happened to other people, it didn't happen here, in this street, on the posh Cline estate. It didn't affect the likes of him.

Except today, it did.

"Can I use your phone, please?" she asked. "I need to get hold of the police."

Chapter Twenty-Nine

Anna had spent all her rage, and during their super-early breakfast of burgers, her adrenaline had depleted, leaving her exhausted. She had no energy in her, so when Rusty had suggested chopping Bastard up, Anna had left her to it. She'd watched, though, disturbed by how she'd viewed it dispassionately, shutting his screams out. She *had* imprinted the blood in her mind, though. So much of it, spurting with every beat of his heart. Until it hadn't done that anymore, instead oozing, forming puddles on the floor around him. Rusty, in a forensic suit and covered in the red stuff, had released animalistic growls with every slice, screaming at Bastard, saying how much she hated him, how he'd ruined her for anyone else, but that she'd move on once he'd been dumped in the Thames, finally free of him.

Except if she was anything like Anna, she'd still see him in her dreams.

It seemed so long ago now, that torture, but it was only a matter of hours. Time had done some weird kind of magic where it had elongated, perhaps Anna's mind at work to preserve her sanity. Patches of what had gone on seemed to have been erased, but she could vividly recall her part in his torture. Turning that screw on the ring, wanting to twist it quickly so he got crushed to death, then changing her mind, needing him to suffer more. She'd felt she owed it to Lacey, Shania, and Rusty to make him pay for hours, make him afraid, like they had been. And she owed it to herself.

What she struggled with was, how could she be a good mother, a good person, if she'd been willing to do that? To harm another human being to such a degree. Did she have something in common with Valandra in that regard? That woman had loved Anna like her own, yet *she'd* done despicable things.

Maybe I should go and see Vic like George said. Pick through it all. Learn to like myself after this.

She'd had a shower at the warehouse, putting on a tracksuit—there had been quite a few of them on a shelving unit, which told her many deaths occurred there and many people needed a change of clothes. What would once have scared and revolted her had become acceptable. The twins did what they had to do, and if it meant wankers like *him* got killed, then the world was a better place for it. Did she have some of her father's and uncle's traits in her after all, to be able to view this so impassively? Was she, underneath it all, like *them*? Would Harper be affected?

At half eight, George and Greg had taken her to the salon flat, and she'd put on her own things, stuffing her hair up in a messy bun and quickly putting makeup on. The change of outfit had put her mind on a different level—she was back to being Anna, the manager of Under the Dryer, her secrets hidden away from the staff and customers. It had helped to distance herself from the horrors of the night, to put it in a box labelled RETRIBUTION AND FREEDOM and dive into the life she wanted, where she'd be a success, happy.

Will had gone to collect Harper, George telling him to buy a proper car seat along the way—George wanted her to have driving lessons, saying they'd get her a car so she could take Harper to Margate for little holidays. Why he'd been so insistent on that location she didn't know, but she was so grateful to him and his brother for looking after them that she'd agreed—*and* she was relieved Greg wasn't dead.

She'd gained a second wind, opening the salon and going about her day as usual. Harper had gone all silly when he'd seen her, his gummy smile wide, and she'd popped him in the playpen so he was close to her. George and Greg had gone home to get some sleep, and as for Rusty? They'd be meeting up tomorrow. The relief that Rusty hadn't become pregnant had given Anna some measure of peace, and she hoped the woman had lived a better life than she had since they'd left the Cline house all those years ago.

Someone had replaced the wooden façade on the back door, then fitted a reinforced gate in the yard that needed a keycode to get in. Whoever had tried to break in had been killed, so she could sleep easy in her flat tonight. The sofa had arrived for the clients, and Will sat on it, his eyes drooping, but he'd insisted he'd stay with her until she shut up shop. And maybe she'd like to go out to dinner, her and Harper, his treat?

She'd accepted, despite knowing she'd be even more knackered later. She liked him, he'd been kind, and she sensed he wanted a friend. Maybe they'd share the full depths of their stories at some point, forming a bond through trauma. It'd be nice to have a mate she could rely on.

The world spun on, everyone else around her oblivious as to how she'd spent the night. She chatted to customers while she cut their hair, put on a front, something she'd learned to do since she'd gone to live with Nan and Grandad Barker. She'd continue to do that for the rest of her life, which started today.

Will winked at her.

She was safe now.

Chapter Thirty

After a day at work functioning on no sleep, Janine sighed and looked around. Her team worked on finding someone who'd left a dead premature baby at a local church, CCTV throwing up nothing, no leads revealing themselves. It had been harrowing to attend the scene, Jim crying at the sight of the naked little mite, Janine not far behind him. She didn't usually show such emotions in front of her colleagues, but when her DS had walked away, unable to stand it anymore, his face in his hands, she'd nearly lost it. She'd left Colin alone to deal with his emotions and studied the pews, searching for anything that would give them a clue.

Nothing.

She stood and went to the whiteboard, reading the scant information, sighing because they had fuck all.

"Anything?" she asked.

Everyone shook their heads.

"Go home. I know it's only four o'clock, but it's been a bloody tough day, and we need to distance ourselves from this. It's too much."

Everyone got up, packing their things away, and within two minutes she stood alone with Colin.

"I'm nipping to the chippy on the way to yours," she said. "Want anything?"

"Yeah. It'll save the wife cooking. I'll text to let her know not to bother. It'll get me some brownie points."

"Oh dear, have you pissed her off again?"

"I didn't help hang her curtains last night, so I'm in the doghouse."

"Then fib and say you've bunked off early to get it done."

"That's a bit underhand."

"Sometimes, you've got to be." She smiled.

They got going, and she pushed the baby out of her mind. She'd had to keep a rein on her emotions all day—they'd been hypersensitive, given what else had gone on, and she couldn't afford for them to come spilling out, not in front of Colin. At the chippy, they ordered their dinner, and while they waited, she glanced outside. Cameron sat in his car, giving her the thumbs-up, and she laughed.

She dropped Colin home and went to her house. Dished the food up and ate without conversation. Cameron let her be, and she was grateful for it. She should be in bed by rights, catching up, but she'd gone past the need for rest, her mind oddly alert. Her muscles ached, though.

"I suppose we should have a discussion." She'd rather get the elephant in the room out of the way: her, a copper, endorsing the sort of thing that had happened and her part in it.

"Hmm, we haven't had a chance to talk about everything," Cameron said. "What happened to you in the night? I mean, you went into some kind of manic trance. Are you okay?"

She nodded. "Much better now he's dead. You already know I walk on the dark side with the twins, so it didn't shock you, but do you have any questions? Like how I can do that?"

"No, I get it. I've told you before, I'm a nasty bastard for The Brothers, but that's a different side of me. What's next? And I don't mean us, we've sorted that, one step at a time. I'm referring to you. Can you move on now?"

"No. There's someone I need to sort. Valandra."

He nodded. "Can't say I blame you. Talk to the twins?"

"Hmm." She'd toyed with it all day in between grieving for that baby. Getting a message inside the nick to some lag who was in for life, so killing someone and adding to her sentence wouldn't make much odds. It was easily done, but she couldn't be the one to make the offer. It might come back to bite her on the arse later.

She'd accessed the file to add that no further sightings of Bastard had occurred at the salon, that he hadn't answered the door when she'd called at his address, and while she'd been at it, she'd found out where Valandra was—if anyone checked what she'd been looking at, she'd say she'd wanted to ensure Valandra hadn't been released and was working with Bastard to bother Anna.

She took her phone out and messaged the twins. Gave them the name, prisoner number, and location.

GG: CONSIDER IT DONE.

They'd somehow get payment to their chosen killer, maybe ask a family member to send the funds over in increments so a large sum wasn't picked up, creating suspicion, something that could be linked as a payment for an organised hit. Whoever it was would have enough to buy their toiletries, cigarettes, and treats for a good while to come.

She put her phone down and stood. If she ripped the plaster off now, it'd be over and done with and she wouldn't have to coil herself up with nerves anymore. "I need to show you something before we move forward."

She undid the buttons of her blouse.

"Steady on," Cameron said on a laugh.

"No, this is important. Just sit there and shut up for a minute."

She undressed, revealing the bite and whip scars—she'd been bitten so hard the teeth had broken the skin. Photos had been taken that night at the police station, and the teeth imprints matched Valandra and David. She stood in all her vulnerability and stared Cameron straight in the eye, the only person since then to have seen her body with the light on.

"This is me," she said. "And no, the cuffs don't match the collar. I dye my hair." She forced herself to be serious. "I'll carry those people around with me forever, inside and out. I've learned not to see them in the mirror, to pretend they're not there, but every so often I get a good look, and it all comes crashing back. This is why I'm spiky, and rude, and overbearing, and obnoxious, because I have to protect myself from being hurt. I couldn't let anyone past that outer shell. I'm damaged goods, a woman who's tried to live her life as normally as she can, but on the darkest nights, when the memories creep out of the walls, I'm Rusty again. Scared. Hurting. Tired. I have nightmares. I relive it in my dreams. I spend the next day barking at everyone. And the worst thing of all, I'm a bent copper like David— and I don't even care anymore."

Her thought from years ago came back. Maybe she was more like Mum than she realised, too. Her moods, cold one minute, overly warm the next, and every other emotion in between.

Cameron stood and traced one of the bites on her breast with a fingertip. It wasn't sexual, more like his way to show her that if he could touch them, they weren't repulsive to him. He didn't display any signs of pity, only admiration.

"You're beautiful no matter what you show everyone else. I like you spiky."

She laughed, nervous. This was the most open she'd ever been. It wasn't as bad as she'd feared, and maybe that was because of who she'd displayed herself to. "I wasn't always like this. Once upon a time I was soft-hearted. Innocent."

"We all were, but life happens. We'll get through this," he said. "I'm not going anywhere."

And she believed him. At last, she trusted a man with her heart.

Chapter Thirty-One

*R*usty couldn't go to uni. She couldn't follow her dream. Instead, she had to look after her mother who'd come out of hospital in a bit of a mess. Tests had confirmed her liver and kidneys were on the verge of packing up. Mum had refused to stay in, saying if she was going to die it'd be on her own terms. Far from feeling sorry for her, Rusty had experienced a horrible surge of hatred—this woman, who was supposed to have cared for her, had left her to grow up without a proper guiding light, and now, she expected her to give up the next however long to nurse her while she died.

Yet another responsibility heaped on Rusty that she hadn't asked for.

But she got on with it. Caring for Mum gave her time to process what had happened in that evil house. The long days of Mum sleeping (in between insisting she needed sips of vodka), meant Rusty cleaned the house out of boredom, her mind wandering.

When the police had arrived at the old man's house on Cline, everything had turned into a flurry of activity. A couple of detectives had spoken to her, Anna taken away by a woman from social services who'd looked after her until her real mother's family could be located. Questions, so many questions, and she'd answered them honestly. She'd told them about the cameras, Valandra erasing the footage, which role each of the evil trio had played. What Valandra had expected Rusty to do. All of it.

"There's a letter in the U-bend under the sink in the flat," she'd said. "From Shania Peterson. She lived at seventy-eight Windermere Gardens, was eighteen. Please make sure you get hold of her mum, promise me."

The statement had continued at the police station. Rusty had watched the comings and goings, noted the way things worked, struck by how seeing it in real life was so different from reading the textbooks. She'd slept for a while, meals provided, then the statement had begun again. Many hours after she'd entered the station, she'd left it, dropped off at an empty, messy house, Mum still in hospital. Red letters on the mat. No electricity. She'd had a cold bath because there had been no gas to heat the boiler either. Found the hundred pounds she'd hidden in her shoe, safe from Mum's clutches. Instead of buying clothes, she'd bought shopping and put a few quid on the leccy meter. Visited the hospital, where Mum had been for ages.

Life could change on you in an instant, she'd discovered that. Her perhaps selfish desire to save herself and run away from her life to university had been stamped on with a heavy boot. Until release had come this morning—and she felt bad for feeling that way. Mum had died a month after coming home. Life was so unfair, giving her shitty parents, and now, she'd missed the deadline to move into uni halls, Mum's death too late for Rusty to run away and lick her wounds. She'd returned the student loan when it had become clear she wouldn't be going but wished she'd kept it. She had a funeral to pay for.

Once Mum's body had been taken, Rusty went round to see Dad. Knocking on his door and telling him his ex-wife had died was one of the most surreal experiences. She'd imagined speaking to him some other way, maybe getting up the courage to go up to him in the pub, telling him she didn't expect anything off him except a bit of conversation—maybe then he'd have accepted her into his life. But once again, fate had other ideas, and here she was, staring at his muddy-brown hair, his pale-blue eyes, not knowing how he'd take the news.

"Well, it was a long time coming." He leaned on the jamb. "I mean, she never did know when to call it a night where booze was concerned. That's why I left her, see. Always fucked off her face, she was."

"And you left me with her."

He shrugged. "Didn't need the baggage. How's life treating you, eh?"

"Pretty shit, actually. I couldn't go to uni. Had to look after Mum."

"What do you want to go to uni for? Fucking trumped-up cow."

"I wanted to do better than you two. Do some good in the world. Make sure kids like me don't suffer—or they at least get the justice they deserve. But you wouldn't know anything about that, would you."

"Less of the gob, you." He frowned. "Anyway, is that it? You've told me about your mother, so jog on."

"I can't afford the funeral. Thought you might want to help, seeing as you were married to her and everything."

"I divorced her. She's fuck all to do with me now. Though I s'pose I could organise a whip-round at the pub she drank at."

"Thanks."

She'd said it sarcastically, but he hadn't seemed to notice. With so many things to say, yet nothing to say at all, she walked off, going home. She stuck some cheap noodles in a saucepan and boiled them on the hob. Thought about all those unpaid bills, the debts, the funeral costs.

She'd have to get a job.

She ate, mulling over her options, then struck on an idea. It could work, and if she was good enough, she'd climb the ladder and be a success some other way. Eventually move out of this shithole and get a mortgage. Right some wrongs. Break free of who she was now, become someone else. Same name, different personality.

She nodded. Smiled. At last, she could move on.

Couldn't she?

Chapter Thirty-Two

The banging of cups against the balcony banisters always signalled something was about to happen. Valandra, on her way up the stairs to her cell after collecting a new book from the library, kept her head down. Whoever was about to get hurt, or if a riot had been organised, she didn't want to be involved. She'd never been 'in the know' here, people giving her a wide berth for the most part, although some picked on her, disgusted by what she'd done. That she'd tried to put it right back then didn't matter in their eyes. She was a sick pervert, and that's all there was to it.

She reached her cell and walked inside. At recreation time, the doors stayed open, so she sat on her bottom bunk and thought about Anna. What was she doing now? Was she happy?

Valandra had been having therapy, and she'd finally got a handle on her childhood and how it had affected her brain. The day she'd come to the realisation that she'd suffered with her mental health but hadn't known there was a problem had been the turning of her new leaf. With session after session, she'd viewed her actions through a different lens, cringing at how easily she'd fallen for David's and Sidney's charms, how they'd chosen someone like her, someone desperate to belong somewhere and be important to them. Loved. Cared for.

Her penchant for sadism in the bedroom had gone too far. She'd allowed herself to become immersed in a terrible game—needing it, wanting it. She'd played it well, even when she'd realised living with David wasn't good for her, but she'd carried on anyway. Her photography, the semi-fame, the big house—she hadn't wanted to give it up. But her thoughts had plagued her enough that she'd had to help Anna.

Now, here she was, locked up, no one to call her own. How strange to be a good person these days and be denied everything nice people had. She wished she'd been good before and hadn't been so scarred from her upbringing—or, she knew now, selfish and spoiled, wanting more and more attention when really, her parents had given her enough. She'd killed them because she'd felt wronged, when in fact, in the scant time they had free after working on the farm, they'd given it all to her.

What a horrible child she must have been.

If she'd been normal, she wouldn't have been in the bar that night and met those evil brothers. Maybe she'd live in a lovely house with a caring husband who didn't mind that she couldn't have children. She could be free and happy.

The 'maybe' trips were a fool's errand. She'd had to deal with what had gone on and accept her part in it, understand it and herself. She'd become part of a survivor's group, the rules dictating that everyone left their personal feelings outside the door and treated each other with respect while in a session. For those hours, she could pretend they were all her friends, that they didn't really hate her, and life inside was more bearable then.

Peacock, her cellmate, walked in. She frowned, glanced over her shoulder, then walked back out.

The clanging cups banged on.

While Peacock only tolerated Valandra, they did spend time in the cell together at recreation by choice—not everyone wanted to go into the yard or watch the television. They were both avid readers (something Valandra thought she'd never be) and more often than not opted to lie on their beds, engrossed in their novels.

Peacock leaving the cell like that wasn't normal.

Valandra got up to peek out. She leaned on the doorframe and assessed the situation. Women ringed the walkway on this, the second floor. Security personnel, as they liked to be called here, kept watch. Peacock had gone down to the ground level, just visible through the net that caught any prisoners who had a mind to leap over the metal banisters and end it all. She spoke to someone then glanced up.

Unnerved, Valandra retreated into the cell and boiled the kettle in case she needed a weapon. She sat on the bed again, and a loud whistle went up, then jeering, cheers, and more banging of the cups. It reached an uncomfortable crescendo, and she closed her eyes, the bubbling of the kettle barely audible. She sensed rather than heard the door closing, the chaotic sounds dulled somewhat, and opened her eyes.

Bentley, one of the lifers, stood there. She held her own kettle, steam rising from the spout. The blonde smiled her demented smile, one that had always churned Valandra's stomach.

"Got a message for you."

Oh God…

She knew what that meant.

"Who…who from?" Which prisoner had she offended *now*? She was so tired of this. Had she said something out of turn at the last survivor meeting?

"Someone on the outside."

Valandra blinked, taking that in. Shit, had *he* been released? Was it *him*? "Have you got a name?"

"The leaders of Cardigan on behalf of someone called Rusty? I see by your face you know who

323

that is. Sounds like your chickens have finally come home to roost. A long time coming if you ask me. I know what you did, you filthy piece of scum."

Bentley clicked a button to release the kettle lid. She came closer, and Valandra scooted backwards on the bunk, her spine touching the wall. Enclosed like this beneath the top bed, she couldn't breathe, panic dragging her under.

"The other one died yesterday," Bentley said. "So there's just you left."

She flung the water at Valandra, and it hit her full in the face. Scorching heat permeated her skin, and she knew what else was in that water. Sugar. Bentley had created what was known as a napalm. Valandra clawed at her face, wanted to rip her skin off, which was spongy beneath her fingertips. Mushy. Bentley dragged her off the bed and dumped her on the floor. Eyelids stuck in the down position, Valandra couldn't lift them to see what was going on or whether Bentley had left. A sharp pain lanced her side, then what she imagined was a blood-wet blade pressed against her neck.

"You should know what comes next because you've done it yourself," Bentley said, "except *I* won't fuck it up like you did."

The burning on her face intensified, worse than the one in her side, and she screamed. She reached out blindly to bat Bentley away, but the woman gripped her wrists together and held them low.

"Night-night, bitch."

Chapter Thirty-Three

*A*lcohol spiralled through her. Eyes closed, Anna danced in one of Manchester's nightclubs in Albion Wharf, the city her home since the police had taken her away that dreadful night. She'd been living with her real mother's family. Nan and Grandad Barker had taken her in seemingly without question, all smiles, but the grumbles had started soon after when the light of the police and social services no longer shone on them. Sadly, their care hadn't exactly been the best, hadn't erased the memories, the fears. She hadn't Googled about the case, and Nan and Grandad said that was probably for the best, considering. They'd looked at each other funny then, but Anna had shrugged it off.

It was clear her mother's parents didn't really know how to parent. They'd fed her, clothed her, got her into school, but it was as if they were a sandwich short, Anna basically bringing herself up. No wonder they hadn't noticed that her mother, Lacey, had been missing until a couple of weeks had gone by. They were party people—the same as Anna was now—more interested in having a laugh than taking proper responsibility.

Anna had avoided going down the rabbit hole on the case. Wasn't it better that she erased that part of her life and started again? She'd tried, but recollections always came back, reminding her of the big house she'd lived in, all her pretty clothes, her toys. The notes with Shania, she'd never forget them, and going into that old man's house with Rusty was a particularly sharp memory.

She drank to blot it out.

Her studies had gone downhill once she'd entered mainstream school. Valandra had one good thing going for her, she'd been an excellent teacher. Anna hadn't cared enough anymore to learn, drifting through life, confused, stuck with a family that, now she came to think about it, she should never have been placed with. Didn't social services do proper checks? Surely they'd seen Nan and Grandad weren't decent role models. But it had been that or the care system, so Anna supposed she ought to be grateful.

The song changed, and she jumped up and down, singing to the words. She'd come here by herself, didn't need friends, didn't even want them, which was odd, because that had been all she'd wanted when living on Cline.

Funny how your priorities changed.

She danced until the main lights went on. Groaned at the thought of turning up at work tomorrow, hungover, her head splitting, yet she did it day after day. Having to listen to customers giving her their life story while she cut their hair. When she'd reached the point where she'd had to pick her college options, Nan had encouraged her into hairdressing.

"People will always need a haircut, so that'd be your best bet. Then you can do mine for free." She'd laughed, phlegm crackling in her throat from the thousands of fags she'd smoked.

Anna had allowed herself a glimmer of hope back then. Maybe one day she'd own a salon, she'd be the boss, and she'd make something of herself. But when she'd started her first job, that glimmer had doused like Nan's fag end in a puddle. Long hours, an aching back and feet, and endless stories coming her way. The wages were shit, yet here she was, years later at twenty-three, still in the same dead-end position.

She remembered being happy, even though she'd barely left the Cline house. She remembered having big dreams of becoming an architect. Dad had said she could be whatever she wanted to be, although he'd appeared sad, as if her leaving the house to go and study was something he couldn't handle. "A discussion for another day," he'd said, and she'd accepted it.

Now, what she couldn't *accept was how a police officer and a doctor could have been so corrupt. And how she'd come to be. Lacey, lured into the house. Raped. Had Rusty been pregnant when she'd walked out of that house? Did Anna have a sibling somewhere? Or would Rusty have had an abortion? The urge to go back to London gripped her, to find Rusty and see whether she had a brother or sister. To finally talk to someone who knew exactly what had* happened. Someone who understood and could commiserate.

She weaved between partygoers who hung around to finish their drinks. She handed her ticket over and collected her coat, stuffing her arms in the sleeves. Out in the cold street, she wandered down the road behind a gaggle of women who pissed themselves laughing at some joke or other. A tiny part of Anna wished she'd allowed herself to have friends, but friends meant sharing secrets, revealing who she was, that kid in the news all those years ago. Friends meant picking off scabs and revealing the ugly, bloodied flesh beneath.

Round the corner, she joined the queue at the kebab van. She'd stink of garlic tomorrow, and her boss would make some snide remark about her breath, so Anna had to remember to take her mints. The line went down quickly, and she ordered, paying and taking the peach-coloured polystyrene tray. Using the plastic fork provided, she ate as she walked along, thinking about Nan possibly waking when she got in, grumbling about the noise, saying it was about time Anna moved out. And she thought of the four hours of sleep she'd get, the alarm going off too soon, and standing behind a chair at work, smiling and laughing at customers when all she wanted to do was scream.

Life wasn't what she'd imagined it would be. No grand houses had been built to her spec. She hadn't fulfilled her dreams, just coasted along on the current of a life she hadn't wanted, no choice but to take it. Maybe opening all those scars and going to see Valandra in prison would put some ghosts back in their graves. Anna asking the most prominent question, "Why?" Did you even love me? Have you missed me?

Maybe it was time for a fresh start.

She finished her kebab and dumped the tray in the bin. Wobbled her way to the taxi rank and waited with a load of other people. She couldn't afford to keep living like this, giving Nan her keep then wasting the rest on boozy nights out. She existed in a fog half the time, the alcohol still in her system from the day before, topped up in the pub as soon as she'd finished work. Then it was home, shower, dressed up to the nines, and she hit the pubs, always ending up in a club. Something had to give.

A few cabs came by and collected those waiting, leaving Anna standing alone, only a streetlamp for company. A man walked along, his head down, hands in coat pockets. He looked like he'd lost a bob or two in his life journey, his skin pasty, his ill-fitting clothes too big. He stood behind her, and she paid him no mind — he was only waiting for a taxi.

"Is your name Anna?" he asked.

Oh God, had she shagged him? She'd swear she wasn't into older men, but when she got so sozzled she couldn't see, it was likely she'd copped off with someone she now couldn't remember. She turned to face him, stepping back to put space between them. "Err, yes?"

"Um, you might not remember me, but I'm your uncle."

She stared, searching his face for signs of it being Lacey's brother, but he was away in the army and wasn't as old. Her sluggish mind, addled by alcohol, couldn't keep up, then suddenly, it cottoned on.

No, it couldn't be him. He was dead. Wasn't he?

"I…" He swallowed. "I haven't been honest. I knew you were Anna. I've been looking for you since…since I came out of prison. I, um, I followed you from the club."

"Fuck off," she snapped, her nerves spiking, skin turning ice-cold. "This isn't funny. My uncle's dead."

He laughed, more like a chuff of air. "I didn't die. She cut my cheek, not my throat." He lifted a finger to point out a scar. "Didn't anyone tell you?"

She ran, heading for the next street. She was hours too late to get the last tram, but she'd peg it to the next taxi rank instead, desperate to get away from him. This couldn't be happening. He couldn't be here. Why hadn't Nan and Grandad said anything? And it made sense now, why they'd looked at each other funny. Why they'd said it was 'probably for the best, considering' when she'd mentioned she wasn't interested in Googling her past.

She glanced over her shoulder, but he wasn't there.

She had to get out of Manchester. Get away from him.

She wasn't safe here now.

Anna's London bedsit wasn't big enough to bring a child up in. She'd done a test this morning, the positive result confirming her fears. What the fuck was she going to do? She didn't even have her own life sorted, let alone taking on the responsibility of a baby's. And who was the father? It could be one of many.

She got ready for work, thankful that even on maternity pay she'd be able to afford this little place, a room in a run-down house full of mould on The Cardigan Estate. She'd save as much of her wages as she could before she had to leave work, and she'd have to cope, because she was having this baby, even though she wasn't ready for it.

She hoped it would be the catalyst that would set her life on the right track. She'd have someone else to look out for, the little person's needs coming before her own. She could stop wallowing in self-pity and carve a new existence. But first, she needed to visit Valandra.

It was Anna's day off. She worked Saturdays and took Mondays off instead. She'd received her visiting order, at first pleased Valandra had agreed to see her, then worried the woman had an ulterior motive.

She took a bus to Ashfield, Surrey, then a taxi to HMP Bronzefield, entering with a riot of butterflies in her belly. It took time to go through the checks, and they provided a locker for her handbag. At last, she went into an open-plan visiting room. Small children sat in a play area, refreshments available across the way. She switched her attention to the prisoners and other people visiting, casting her gaze around.

She hadn't expected her to look so haggard. So old. The mirage that had remained in Anna's head was of a poised, elegant woman, her hair usually in a chignon or French pleat, her clothes perfect. Here, she could pass as some over-the-hill, down-on-her-luck drifter, hair lacklustre, skin sallow, grey bags beneath her eyes.

Anna approached, asking herself for the umpteenth time if she should be here. Valandra stood, her eyes watering, and she held out her hands for a hug then dropped them to her sides.

"No, of course you wouldn't want to cuddle me." She sat again, laid her hands on her lap, and dipped her head. "I'm so sorry."

Anna sat. "Sorry you got caught?"

Valandra raised her chin. Stared at her defiantly, then her expression softened, as if she'd reminded herself it wasn't Anna's fault she was in prison. It was hers. "Sorry for how things turned out. I had such high hopes, you know. If it wasn't for Rusty, you and I would have lived together."

"On the run. I wouldn't exactly have had a great life, locked away yet again, and you'd have been caught eventually."

"I suppose."

"I found out Sidney didn't die."

Valandra winced. "No, I…I closed my eyes when I cut him. Thought I'd slit his throat, but clearly, I missed. Silly of me not to check. How did you find out? Did your grandparents tell you everything?"

"No, I didn't want to know, still don't. He…he'd been looking for me since he got out—I take it he only got done for knowing what you and my father were up

to, being complicit in incarcerating women. What was it, a fifteen-year stint, maybe a bit less? Whereas you…unlikely to be let out anytime soon. Anyway, he turned up at a taxi rank when I was pissed out of my head. Introduced himself. I drink—drank—a lot. You three fucked me up."

Valandra cringed. "I'd told myself you'd gone to good people, that you'd grow up without all the baggage."

"I expect you do what you've got to so you don't have to admit any guilt. I mean, helping to keep a child indoors until she was eight…tough thing to come to terms with. But then again, for you to have done that, you must be a nutter and think it's normal."

"I had no choice," Valandra whispered. "Your father—"

"That's it, blame the dead man who can't defend himself. I'm willing to bet, if I get the balls up to Google, it'll tell me a different story. I bet you're dying to tell me your version."

"No. You're better off not knowing. I love you enough to spare you that."

Anna rose. "I won't come back again. You were no mother to me, even though you claim to have wanted to get me out of that house. I don't know what you are. Can't find a name for it. Sometimes, though, I wish *you'd gone along with it all until I was older. Until I became what I wanted to be. I was loved in that house—I never felt as though I wasn't—and to be chucked into a home with a nan and grandad who thought more about having a good time than bringing me up... You ruined me by trying to save me, and I'll never forgive you for it."*

Disturbed by her outburst, how she'd finally acknowledged that she'd have rather stayed with three mental cases than be with her grandparents, she left the room, pausing outside to lean on the wall and cry. The tears, hot and heavy, scored down her cheeks, and she wondered, if she'd have preferred such a life, whether her father's genes ran through her stronger than she'd thought.

Repulsed by that, she prepared herself to leave, promising her unborn child that she'd do her best, be honest, and never break the law.

Never be like them.

Chapter Thirty-Four

GG: It's done.

Janine: Any repercussions?

GG: Not that we're aware of.

Janine: I expect the DCI will inform me.

GG: Then you know what to do.

Janine: Yeah, put on my shocked face.

GG: We're here if you need to talk to us.

Janine: I know, but I have Cameron now.

GG: About time.

Janine: Fuck off.

"I've often thought about you," Janine said in Bumble's Café, a latte in front of her and a slice of carrot cake she didn't think she could stomach.

Anna nodded. "Same. Difficult not to."

It was awkward, this. They shared a common bond, experiences, and memories, yet Janine couldn't think of a thing to say in relation to it.

"Maybe this wasn't such a good idea," she said. "You don't know the half of what went on, so I'm not going to know what subject to broach and what to stay away from. I don't blame you for shielding yourself from it, but meeting me like this, where it's just us… A bit too raw?"

Anna nodded, seeming lost without her son. George and Greg had taken him off for a walk in the buggy.

"I *can* tell you something, though." Janine worried about the revelation. Valandra had been Anna's mother for eight years, and she wasn't sure how Anna felt about her. "But it might come as a bit of a shock."

Anna laughed, the sound carrying a nervous lilt. "I've had so many shocks lately, one more won't matter. Just say it and be done with it."

"Valandra died earlier today."

Anna's face paled.

Shit.

"I'm sorry," Janine said. "For your loss. If she, you know, if you still loved her."

"I didn't. I don't. She was dead to me that day I visited her in prison."

"You did?"

"Hmm. I wanted to...I don't know *what* I wanted if I'm honest. But I had to go, and in a way I'm glad I did, because I realised I wanted nothing to do with her. How did she die? I hope she didn't go peacefully in her sleep."

"She was murdered."

Anna smiled. "So someone finally got it done. Good. There must have been loads of people waiting for their chance all these years."

"*I* got it done." Janine waited for the penny to drop.

"What? How?"

"The twins sorted it." Janine sipped some coffee.

"They can even get to people *inside*?"

"No one's safe."

Anna pondered that for a moment. "I'm beginning to see that. What…how did they do it?"

"Another prisoner burned her face, stabbed her in the side, then slit her throat."

"Fitting."

"Hmm."

Anna lifted her slice of Victoria sponge and took a bite. Chewed. Swallowed. "Lovely, this."

Janine knew what she was doing. Either deflecting to hide her feelings or showing that she considered the cake more important than a mother figure. Which it was in a way, but in others, not so much. The mental and emotional scars couldn't be erased with the taste of sponge, jam, and cream.

Janine bit into her carrot cake. "This is lovely, too."

They smiled at each other, an understanding born between them; they'd continue to live in the best way they knew how, covering the scars with cakes and coffee and inane chatter, with sunrises and sunsets, the daily grind.

It was all they knew how to do.

Chapter Thirty-Five

Nessa stood in the crematorium, people belting out 'Abide with Me' as if that would show God they were good people and gave a shit that Dickie Feathers had died. She dabbed at her dry eyes with a tissue, nodding to Jordy's wife who'd been badgering Nessa for days about where her husband and his friends might be. Bringing up the fact the lock-up had been torched. Nessa had snapped that she wasn't the fucking Oracle and had her own problems to deal with. She'd felt bad, but the more distance she put between herself and Dad's friends' situation the better.

Mum lifted a handkerchief to her eyes, blotting tears Nessa suspected were for herself, all the years she'd put up with that man. Dad's stuff had been packed up the day after he'd died, Mum taking it all to the charity shop. Not one thing of his remained, and she'd even got rid of the leather suite he'd coveted, opting for a cheap fabric effort to replace it until she moved up north.

The service came to an end, and Nessa led the mourners from the building, pondering on whether bricks burned to ash or if the coffin would be driven away somewhere instead, the bricks removed. George hadn't given her the finer details, and she didn't want them. As far as she was concerned, the arsehole known as the Beast no longer existed, and that meant she'd now have a happier life.

Mum got into one of the black cars, the driver taking her to the wake. Nessa, caught up in thanking people for coming, played the part of a mourning daughter. As the last few people wandered off to make their way to the Noodle, she caught sight of someone half hiding behind a tree. She sucked in a breath. Miss Marlborough, long black hair gleaming, stepped out into full view and tiptoed across the grass, likely so her high heels didn't dig in and get dirty.

"Nessa," she said in her posh voice, stopping in front of her. "I'm sorry for your loss."

"Don't be," she snarled, then wished she hadn't revealed her true feelings.

"Whatever do you mean?"

"Nothing. I'm a bit all over the place today. Ignore me. Can I help you?"

"Um, this is a bit delicate, but I was wondering when the will is being read."

"I don't know if he even has one."

"Oh, he does." Marlborough smiled. "Your father and me—"

"I know."

"Our son—"

"So it's true, then. Mum wasn't imagining things."

"No. Poor woman. I do feel bad."

"Don't."

Marlborough's fake eyelashes fluttered. "Pardon me?"

"She had plenty of chances to walk away but didn't. She…didn't treat me in the best way, and neither did Dickie, so I've got no time for her."

"I'm aware of how he behaved with your mum, and I'm really sad about it. I did try to talk your father round, to be kinder to her, but he…had a specific way of looking at things."

"You can say that again." Nessa toed the path.

"Listen, we don't need the money, so if he's left us anything other than what we're due regarding our office—"

Office?

"—we're happy to let you keep it. I really don't want your mother on my back, although I can understand her feelings towards me, of course I can. It's just that there's something you don't know, and now that your dad's gone, his 'business dealings' might he mentioned at the will reading, and I don't think your mother will be pleased. Maybe you could have a word with the solicitor so our part in things is mentioned to us separately so she doesn't know?"

"I'm not sure how it all works, but I'll try."

"And we need some help on another matter. A 'keep it in the family' sort of thing."

Nessa frowned, maggots of unease writhing in her stomach. "What do you mean?"

"We…we have a racket going and need three people to run it. There's only the two of us now."

Nessa held a hand up. "No. I work for The Brothers. I absolutely can't get involved."

"They don't need to know. I mean, they've been unaware of it all this time, so…"

Nessa thought about it. How she could discover the ins and outs yet remain in the twins' good books. "What does the racket involve?"

"Drugs. We could do with a proper chat if you're interested in taking on your father's role." Marlborough glanced around, seemingly relieved they were alone. "Something awful happened, and if Dickie had been here, he'd have handled it. Instead, we had to do what we thought was best. He said you're clever, loyal, and we can trust you. We need you to…to have a word with someone, stop them from talking. Persuade them, if you like, to see things from our point of view."

"I'm not like him, I'm not a bloody heavy!"

"But you're tough, and you can be scary when you want to be, he told me that. Please, we've got no one else to turn to."

Nessa sighed. "What happened?"

"A druggy came to buy her usual. She didn't have the money and kicked up a bit of a stink when we wouldn't hand anything over on tick. She threatened to go to the police. She was pushed, and she fell onto her stomach. She was pregnant. Long story short, she had the baby in our office, and it… It was dead when it came out. Premature. Chesney said he'd deal with it. He took it away."

"The baby left in the *church*?" Nessa gaped at her. "The one the police are all over?"

Marlborough nodded. "Yes."

"Where's the mother?"

Marlborough bit her lip. "Unfortunately, she's still with us."

"*What*?"

"We chained her up. My boy has tried so hard to be like his father, but he hasn't quite hit the mark. Will you help us? *Please*? Help your brother if you don't want to help me?"

Nessa's mind spun. This was more than she could handle. Why the *fuck* did this woman think *she'd* know what to do? "You should take her to the police station or a hospital."

"And risk her telling them who we are and what happened? It's gone too far now. It's Chesney's fault that baby died because he *pushed* her."

"You could have got rid of all the drugs, taken her to the hospital, and if she'd grassed you up, there'd be nothing in your office when the police came round. You could have said she was off her face, needing a fix, and thought you were suppliers, that she went into labour on her own— and you could have made out she was lying if she refuted that."

"See? This is why we need you. That's exactly what Dickie would have done. He wouldn't let emotions cloud his judgement."

Nessa reckoned this woman was nuttier than squirrel shit. She'd explained the circumstances as though it was nothing more than the inconvenience of a burst pipe under the sink. Yet this could amount to murder—*that poor baby*— and holding someone against their will. Long sentences in the nick.

She'd have to agree so she could free the woman. "Okay, I'll help, but not today. I've got to get to the wake."

"Tomorrow morning, before the pub opens?"

Nessa nodded. "I'll need your address."

Marlborough took a phone out of her bag and handed it over. "I got this ready in case. Only use it for our business. Mine and Chesney's numbers are already on there, and the office address is in the notes app. If the woman won't agree to keep her mouth shut, if you can just kill her for us, that would be great."

Kill her? What the actual fuck?

Nessa played along. "This is the one and only thing I'm doing for you. I don't want any involvement in your business, you'll have to take on someone else for that. I've got a pub to run, and I don't need the hassle."

Marlborough smiled. "Thank you, darling. See you in the morning."

She picked her way over the grass again to a path on the other side. Nessa stared after her, gobsmacked. Had Jordy known what Dad he been up to with that woman, selling drugs? Had Mum?

Nessa got into the last black car, the driver waiting for her. She smiled. She'd like nothing more than getting her father's name blackened, even if it *was* after his death. He'd turn in his grave if he could see what she was doing.

The car glided through the streets.

She'd eat, drink, mingle with the mourners, and receive more condolences. Then, tomorrow morning, she'd free that poor woman then tell the twins everything.

She held back laughter.

Fuck you again, Dickie Feathers!

To be continued in *Reflect*,
The Cardigan Estate 24

Printed in Great Britain
by Amazon

34145166R00202